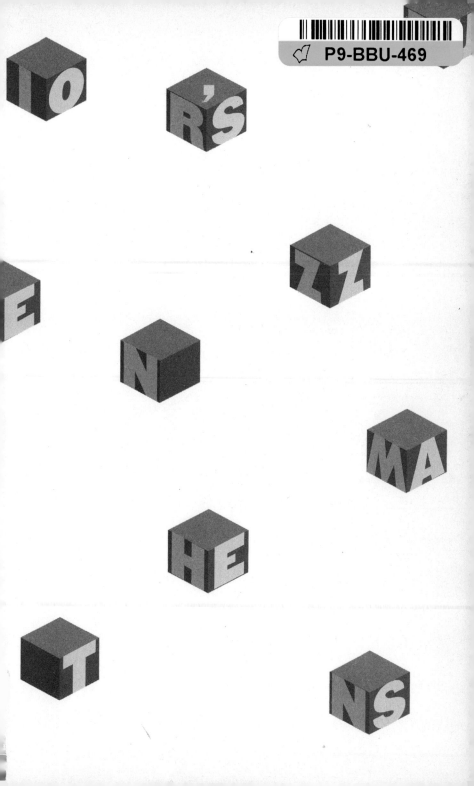

Puzzle your way through these

other Winston Breen books:

The Puzzling World of Winston Breen

The Puzzling World of Winston Breen:
The Potato Chip Puzzles

The Puzzling World of
Winston Breen

THE PUZZLER'S MANSION

ERIC BERLIN

G. P. Putnam's Sons
Penguin Young Readers Group

G. P. PUTNAM'S SONS

A division of Penguin Young Readers Group.

Published by The Penguin Group.

Penguin Group (USA) Inc., 375 Hudson Street, New York, NY 10014, U.S.A.

Penguin Group (Canada), 90 Eglinton Avenue East, Suite 700, Toronto, Ontario M4P 2Y3, Canada

(a division of Pearson Penguin Canada Inc.).

Penguin Books Ltd, 80 Strand, London WC2R 0RL, England.

Penguin Ireland, 25 St. Stephen's Green, Dublin 2, Ireland (a division of Penguin Books Ltd.).

Penguin Group (Australia), 250 Camberwell Road, Camberwell, Victoria 3124, Australia

(a division of Pearson Australia Group Pty Ltd).

Penguin Books India Pvt Ltd, 11 Community Centre, Panchsheel Park, New Delhi—110 017, India.

Penguin Group (NZ), 67 Apollo Drive, Rosedale, Auckland 0632, New Zealand

(a division of Pearson New Zealand Ltd).

Penguin Books (South Africa) (Pty) Ltd, 24 Sturdee Avenue, Rosebank,

Johannesburg 2196, South Africa.

Penguin Books Ltd, Registered Offices: 80 Strand, London WC2R 0RL, England.

Design by Annie Ericsson. Text set in ITC Century.

Library of Congress Cataloging-in-Publication Data

Berlin, Eric. The puzzler's mansion / Eric Berlin ; [ink drawings by Katrina Damkoehler].

p. cm.—(The puzzling world of Winston Breen ; 3)

Summary: Winston attends a weekend of puzzles at a famous musician's mansion,
but when he and other young guests pursue a thief, they find themselves in big trouble.

Puzzles for the reader to solve are included throughout the text.

[1. Puzzles—Fiction. 2. Robbers and outlaws—Fiction. 3. Musicians—Fiction.
4. Mansions—Fiction. 5. Mystery and detective stories.] I. Damkoehler, Katrina. II. Title.

PZ7.B45335Ptp 2012 [Fic]—dc23 2011031624

ISBN 978-0-399-25697-4

1 3 5 7 9 10 8 6 4 2

For teachers who make a difference.

And while we're on the subject, this book is for
Claire Donohue, Robert Sarli, and Bill Scott.

Also, thanks to Joshua Kosman for his musical expertise,
Lance Nathan for his puzzle assistance,
and Mark Halpin and Francis Heaney, nitpickers extraordinaire.

ABOUT THE PUZZLES IN THIS BOOK

This book contains quite a few puzzles. You can solve them if you want, although you don't *have* to solve them to enjoy the story. Most of the answers can be found in the back of the book. Some of the puzzles are so important to the story, however, that the answer appears on the very next page. You'll see which ones those are when you get to them. Note that you can't really skip those puzzles and come back to them later, because you'll learn the answer almost immediately. Take a few minutes to try them, and then continue reading.

And if you don't want to write in this book, just head over to **www.winstonbreen.com**. There you can download and print out all the puzzles. Happy solving!

WINSTON BREEN HAD never been in trouble before—
not *this* much trouble. Winston's father shook his head. He looked
tired and disappointed. Somehow that was worse than angry.

They were sitting together on the sofa. Winston's mom and his
sister, Katie, were in the kitchen playing a board game and taking
turns glancing over to the living room. His mom looked worried,
while Katie's expression combined sisterly concern with smug satis-
faction that she was not the one in trouble.

Unfortunately, Winston had been summoned to the living room
sofa quite a few times lately.

The problem was this: Winston's social studies teacher, Mr.
Burke, was a walking, talking sleeping pill. Winston had never fully
appreciated the way other teachers made their lessons interesting,
even entertaining. Mr. Burke was not there to entertain them. The
man had said as much on the first day of school: he was there to
teach American history, not to amuse them. And from that day forward, Mr. Burke stood at the front of the room, rocking on his heels
and droning about Lewis and Clark or Plymouth Rock or whatever,

occasionally referring to his notes but otherwise not moving an inch.

Paying attention to this man was impossible. Impossible! The mind was forced to wander, and Winston's mind, as usual, wandered to puzzles. His notebook contained the occasional scribble about the lesson, but mostly it was filled with attempts to anagram Lewis and Clark or Plymouth Rock into funny new phrases. (War Dance Kills! Pluck Thy Room!)

Mr. Burke soon figured out that his students weren't hanging on his every word. He would call on kids to repeat what he'd just said, and when the unfortunate victim could not, he would send a note home to be signed by that kid's parents. Totally unfair.

Winston had received three notes in five weeks. His mother and father were not happy. He tried explaining that Mr. Burke was the most boring teacher on earth, that he *had* to think about more interesting things in order to stay awake. His parents didn't want to hear it. They warned him that his love of puzzles was interfering with his schoolwork, and if it continued, there would be a price to pay.

For a while, everything was fine. Winston paid attention in class and resisted sketching out puzzle ideas. He planted his elbow on his desk, fastened his chin to the palm of his hand, and stared at Mr. Burke, determined not to receive another aggravating note.

And then, after all that, it was *science* class where Winston had his big downfall. Like a boxer who's too focused on an opponent's left jab, Winston got hit with a right hook that he never saw coming.

Science was a perfectly fine class. Mrs. Haider was a short, energetic woman who made her subject seem pretty interesting—way more than Mr. Burke managed, anyway. And twice a week there were labs, which Winston always enjoyed.

His lab partner, by virtue of alphabetical order, was a girl named Pamela Cassetti. She was absent on the day Winston landed in the vice principal's office, and that was probably half the problem right there. If Pamela had been around, Winston might have paid more attention to that day's experiment, which involved pendulums. But, no. Winston's eyes settled on some glass beakers, rinsed out and drying by the sink, close to his lab station. They reminded him of a puzzle he had seen some time ago, and he wondered if could re-create it.

There was plenty of time left to get his experiment done, so he took the three beakers to his table and examined them.

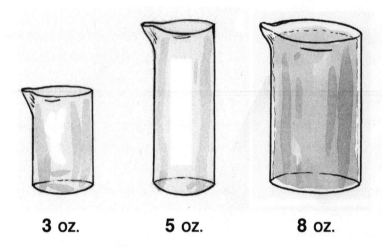

3 oz.   **5 oz.**   **8 oz.**

There are three beakers. One holds 8 ounces and is full of water. The others are empty. One can hold 3 ounces, and the other can hold 5 ounces. None of the beakers have measurements marked on them, so unless a beaker is full, you can't accurately determine how much water is in it. Nonetheless, can you figure out how to measure out exactly 4 ounces of water?

(Answer, page 241.)

He was setting one of the beakers down when Mrs. Haider called out, "Winston, *what* are you doing?" Winston's reaction was to try to hide the beakers, which was dumb, since Mrs. Haider had already seen them. And it was even dumber than *that*, because in his haste to get the beakers back to the sink, he dropped two of them. They seemed to almost float downward, giving Winston plenty of time to gasp and wish himself back in time thirty seconds or so. Then they shattered on the floor.

Mrs. Haider was on him at once, a screaming typhoon of a lady. She asked very loudly why Winston was playing with the beakers in the first place. She wondered at the top of her lungs whether Winston had lost his mind. She yelled at him to grab a broom and a dustpan, clean up every last shard of glass, and then get himself down to the vice principal's office, where he would become Mr. Rothenberger's problem and she would no longer have to look at him.

Winston had never been in Mr. Rothenberger's "hot seat," an orange plastic chair next to the vice principal's desk, and he hoped to never be there again. He received a withering lecture about school property and respect and values, and all sorts of related subjects, until Winston was ready to sign a solemn oath that he would never get in trouble again—not in junior high school, not in high school, not in college. Never. And then Mr. Rothenberger said, "I am going to have to call your parents about this, you understand." Winston slumped in his chair. He had survived Mrs. Haider's screaming and Mr. Rothenberger's lecture, but there were more surprises ahead on this miserable obstacle course.

His father, thankfully, wasn't much for yelling. This evening he didn't seem to have a lecture in him, either. He only shook his head and thought for a long time before saying, "Well, Winston . . . what are we going to do about this?"

"I don't know," Winston replied honestly.

"That makes two of us," said Nathan Breen. "I mean, you'll be paying the school back for the equipment you broke. That much is clear. And there will be a punishment. No video games or television during the week until further notice."

Winston's eyes flicked down. *During the week* was an important concession. That meant he could still have these things over the weekend.

His father continued, "I don't know what to say about your puzzles. I know you love doing them. I know you love creating them. I have always encouraged that. I'm very proud of you, and I'm proud of this ability you have developed." He paused long enough to sigh and shake his head again. "But it is becoming a distraction. Do you see that?"

It would have been hard to miss. "Yes," Winston said.

"What do you plan to do about it?"

"I'm not going to do puzzles as much," he said. That sounded incredible even to him. He looked at his father's face and sensed that more was needed. "And I won't do them in school anymore." That wasn't very convincing, either, so he added, "Not during classes, anyway."

His father stared at him as if trying to decide how much of this to believe. Finally he allowed himself a rueful little smile. "You have to decide who you're going to be, Winston. Your grades aren't as good this year, you're getting these notes home from your teachers—"

Just one teacher, Winston thought but did not say.

"—and now this thing in science class. That brain of yours is everywhere but where it's supposed to be." He gave a final, frustrated toss of his hands. "Only you can change that. Go do your homework." And with that, Nathan Breen got up and went to his office.

Katie, in the kitchen, made a disgusted sound. She must have thought Winston would be grounded, or possibly banished from the house. "Oh, you got so *lucky*," she called out.

She was probably right, but Winston didn't feel lucky.

The dreadful week ended and then it was Saturday. At last, Winston was allowed to watch television and play video games, but he found he didn't want to. He didn't want to solve anything in his puzzle books, either. He was trying to keep puzzles on a low simmer instead of a raging boil.

He wished he could get together with Mal and Jake, his two best friends, but Winston hadn't seen much of them since the start of school. Winston had shared classes with one or both of his friends since first grade—but this year, Mal and Jake had three classes together, while Winston's schedule didn't overlap with theirs at all. Not even for lunch! Worse, his two friends were off in their own orbits. Jake had joined the swim team and was over at the high school for practice almost every afternoon. And Mal had gotten a role in the school play and was busy with rehearsals. Winston was starting to feel like he'd been exiled to a desert island somewhere.

Summer had decided to put its feet up and linger into October. Katie was watching cartoons, and his parents were busy in their own grown-up worlds, his father doing paperwork in his office and his mother sorting clothes in the bedroom. Winston felt restless. He had to get out of here, even if he had nowhere to go.

A few minutes later, he was on his bicycle, pedaling into a warm morning breeze. Aimless, he headed toward the town green, and from there he supposed he would go see Mr. Penrose. The last few times he had visited Penrose's Curio Shop, Penrose had taught him a few things about chess. Maybe he could get another lesson, or maybe he would just explore the shop's crowded shelves and its endless supply of fascinating bric-a-brac. At least he'd be able to talk to somebody.

Penrose greeted him like an old friend, and the two of them chatted about this and that. Winston, intending to ask for a chess lesson, impulsively asked for a game instead. Penrose brought out the board, and soon they were sitting quietly together, Winston with a cold soda nearby.

It didn't take long for Winston to realize this was a mistake. Penrose's black pieces performed in elegant harmony, while Winston's white pieces were like sixteen kittens tangled in a ball of yarn. Winston's army was soon shredded, and every possible move looked like it would only lead to further disaster. Penrose wasn't even paying attention to the board at this point. He read a magazine and occasionally rose from his chair to help a customer. Hardly a word had passed over the chessboard in the last hour, except when one man, holding a brass lamp he had just purchased, looked at the game, patted Winston on the shoulder, and said, "Good luck, kid."

Winston shook his head. What had made him think he could win this game, or even be competitive, after five brief chess lessons? He extended a finger and knocked his king over, officially resigning the game.

Mr. Penrose offered a hand. "A good game."

Winston shook it but said, "No, it wasn't."

"Oh, now. Don't be hard on yourself," Mr. Penrose said. "You handled the opening moves reasonably well. You tried to control the middle of the board. It's clear that you understand the basics. You see when an opponent's piece is about to make a threat, but you don't always see when two pieces are working in tandem. And that's fine. It's early days, Winston. With practice, you will improve. I can give you some books if you wish to study on your own."

"Maybe," Winston said with a shrug.

Penrose understood that he had been politely rebuffed. "Or perhaps you would prefer this." He reached under his counter and came up with a second chessboard—a smaller one, just six by six.

"What's that, chess for beginners?" Winston asked.

Mr. Penrose smiled and said, "Some people prefer to teach the game on a smaller board. I'm not of that mind myself. But I thought you might like a little chess puzzle." He placed the board on the countertop, reached underneath again, and came back with a handful of chess pieces, all queens. Winston found himself intrigued.

"All you have to do," Mr. Penrose said, "is put these six queens on the chessboard so that none of them are attacking each other. Which means, of course, that none can be in the same row or column, or on the same diagonal. Can you do it?"

(Answer, page 242.)

*　　*　　*

So much for not doing puzzles today. Winston took a few minutes to try out Penrose's challenge and was soon absorbed, sliding queens this way and that around the board. He'd been working for a while when the bell over the door rang and the mailman came in. A moment later, Mr. Penrose, flipping through the junk mail and catalogs, made a little sound, not quite a gasp.

"Are you okay?" Winston asked.

"Oh, yes," Penrose said in a faraway voice. "Everything is fine." He was gazing at a small red envelope. Now he reached for a letter opener.

Winston watched as Penrose became engrossed by the contents of the envelope. After a moment, he began sliding queens around the chessboard again, pretending to be interested in the puzzle even when Mr. Penrose said, "Huh!" as if some wonderful mystery had just deepened. Winston looked up again to find his old friend smiling cryptically at him.

"What?" Winston said.

Mr. Penrose raised a finger: *Wait a minute—I'm thinking.* After a moment, he went behind the counter and paged through a small, leather-bound book. Finding what he wanted, he picked up the phone and dialed.

Someone on the other end answered, and Mr. Penrose said, "Norma! It's good to hear your voice. It's Arthur Penrose. Yes, quite well. Thank you. Is he in?" There was a brief silence, and then Penrose said, "Richard! How are you. Yes? Oh, here, too. I'm glad to hear it. I wanted to ask about this invitation. Does it mean what it says? It's quite a departure from the usual thing. . . ." There was a pause, then Penrose laughed and said, "Well, I'm wondering if the guests strictly need to be relations." He looked at Winston and said, "I have somebody I would like to bring along. Oh, yes. Someone who will truly appreciate what you do. That's okay, then? Excellent. I shall see you in a couple of weeks. Of course, I wouldn't miss it. All right, then. Bye."

Penrose hung up and sat down, as pleased as Winston had ever seen him. Winston had forgotten all about the chessboard. Mr. Penrose wanted to take him somewhere?

"A few weeks ago," Penrose said, "you mentioned how you don't get to see those two friends of yours as frequently anymore. Those two boys."

"Mal and Jake. Yeah," Winston said.

"We haven't really spoken about it since then. But if I may say so, Winston, you seemed rather down about it. And you don't seem all that much improved even today."

Winston frowned, and his eyes dropped to the chessboard. "It hasn't been a good time, I guess. Mal and Jake are busy. . . . School has been hard. . . ." He concluded with a shrug.

"Well, then," said Mr. Penrose, "I may have just the ticket."

"The ticket for what?"

"The ticket to distract you from your current raft of problems, of course." He slid the red envelope across the counter.

Winston was amazed that his curiosity about Penrose's letter was going to be satisfied so soon. He picked up the envelope. It unfolded to reveal a single ornately printed card at its center:

*You are invited to a weekend
of games, puzzles, and amusements
at the home of Richard Overton.
You know where that is, right?
Arrive October 21.
The games start October 22.
Bring the family this time, if you like!
But either way, show up.
Don't make me ask you twice.*

Winston read the invitation three times before saying to Mr. Penrose, "You want me to go to a party with you? A party that lasts all *weekend?*"

Mr. Penrose said, "Normally these events are restricted to invitees only, but you are in luck. For some reason, he's decided to let guests bring their children along. I have no children, so instead I am offering this to you. I think you would find Richard's weekend gatherings to be a lot of fun. And you look like you could use some fun right about now."

"Who is this guy?"

Penrose said, "You've never heard of Richard Overton?"

Winston shook his head.

"He's a musician. He plays the piano," Mr. Penrose said.

"Oh," said Winston. "Is he good?"

Penrose smiled. Winston had the feeling he had just asked a stupid question. "Let me give you a CD," Penrose said. "Take it home and listen to it. You can judge for yourself."

Winston thought, The answer to the question is yes. Richard Overton is a good piano player. But he said, "Okay, sure."

Penrose had a small shelf dedicated to old music. He moved his finger along this, searching, and came up with a particular compact disc.

"Oh, hey," said Winston. "I don't want to take something you're supposed to sell."

Penrose waved a hand. "I don't sell much music, and I have numerous copies of this album. It's my gift to you. I'm sure you'll like it. But whether you like it or not, I *know* you'll enjoy a weekend at Richard's estate."

"His . . . estate?" Winston was starting to get intrigued.

Penrose nodded. "He has a large, beautiful house a couple of hours upstate. And every once in a while, he invites a number of his friends to visit, and he challenges us with puzzles and games that he has created."

"What kind of puzzles?" Winston asked.

"Oh, they're different every time," Penrose said. "My friend Richard is a clever fellow. I think the two of you would get along very well."

Winston looked at the CD. It seemed no different than the handful of classical albums his parents owned. The cover showed a close-up of a pair of hands hovering over a piano keyboard, fingers arched as if about to play something complicated and dramatic.

"How do you know this guy?" he asked.

"My wife was a musician," Penrose said.

"Your wife?"

"She died some years ago."

"Oh," Winston said. He didn't know Mr. Penrose had been married.

"They performed a series of concerts together. This was quite a while back, you understand. In fact, it's probably close to fifty years now. My goodness." Penrose wore a faint and dreamy smile, as if he could still hear the music. "Anyway," he said, "I stayed friendly with Richard even after Rebecca passed away. He knows I've always enjoyed his games." He became more clear-eyed and said, "So will you, Winston, I guarantee it. Ask your parents if you can go. If they have any questions, they can call me."

The whole idea that he might try to walk away from puzzles—even for a day—suddenly seemed ridiculous. A weekend of puzzly games at some famous person's mansion? How could Winston not jump at this?

"Okay. I'll go ask them right now." He thanked his friend for the invitation.

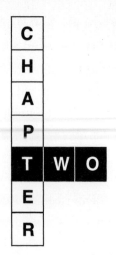

THE MORE WINSTON thought about Penrose's offer, the more excited he got. The entire bicycle ride home, he rehearsed what he was going to say to his parents. Would they let him go to a weekend-long puzzle party so soon after he'd gotten in trouble for solving puzzles? He wasn't sure.

Well, he had to go. He would promise them anything.

He burst into the house, calling out for his parents before the door had shut behind him. "Shhh!" said Katie, from the living room. She was playing a video game with two of her friends, the three of them concentrating on the television screen, where cartoony race cars puttered about. "Dad's working," Katie said. "And Mom's out."

"He's working?" Winston asked. "On a Saturday?" Katie didn't respond, so he knocked on his father's office door and stuck his head in. He was dismissed with a stern look and a wave of the hand. His father was pacing and talking on the phone, clearly in the middle of some urgent problem. Winston closed the door, sighing.

The excitement of Penrose's invitation was still with him, and now it had nowhere to go. Winston thought about calling Mal or Jake, and was just about to pick up the phone when he remembered his father was using it. Perfect. He really needed his own cell phone one of these days.

Winston didn't want to watch his sister play video games, so he headed up to his room. He had begun the day not knowing what to do with himself, and now he was right back where he'd started, only this time with a whopper of a story that he couldn't wait to share. Sighing, he grabbed a puzzle magazine. He had said he would back away from puzzles for a while, but this was an emergency. He took a pencil from his desk, threw himself onto his bed, and looked for something he hadn't solved yet.

The answer to each clue below is a palindrome—a phrase that reads the same forward and backward. For instance, the clue "a few intelligent male sheep" would lead to the phrase SMART RAMS. In each answer, the number of words and number of letters in each word is given to you.

1. Pile up kittens

— — — — —   — — — —

2. Run away from Santa's helper

— — — —   — — —

3. Edge of a reflective surface

— — — — — —   — — — —

4. Notice football officials

— — —   — — — — — — — —

5. Doctor's assistants move hurriedly

__ __ __ __ __ __   __ __ __

6. Bone in a robin

__ __ __ __   __ __ __

7. Black-and-white "bear" slept awhile

__ __ __ __ __   __ __ __   __ __ __

8. Students make a mistake

__ __ __ __ __ __   __ __ __ __   __ __

9. Stand up before you cast your ballot, mister

__ __ __ __   __ __   __ __ __ __,   __ __ __

10. Smack friends who join me in exercising

__ __ __ __   __ __ __   __ __ __ __   __ __ __ __

(Answers, page 242.)

Halfway through the puzzle, he remembered the CD from Mr. Penrose. He found it and looked at the case. It was Richard Overton and the Chicago Symphony Orchestra playing Rachmaninoff's Piano Concerto No. 3. Winston wondered why classical composers didn't use proper song titles. It was always Symphony No. 5, followed by Symphony No. 6, which was followed a few years later by, you guessed it, Symphony No. 7. Would it have killed them to come up with some catchier names?

In any event, he liked the name Rachmaninoff. He said it aloud, enjoying the rhythm of it. It sounded like a rubber ball bouncing off the wall, onto the ground, and back into his hand.

Winston popped the disc into his computer, turned up the speakers, and went back to his puzzle. Music filled the room—a piano, backed up by a roomful of strings. It was pleasant enough, and sort of interesting to know that the guy playing the piano was a friend of his friend and someone he might meet soon. But if Penrose thought that Winston would be blown away by the music, then Penrose was going to be disappointed. Winston doubted he would listen to this a second time.

Still, it wasn't bad. Winston let the music play while he continued solving.

A few minutes later, he looked up from his puzzle again. The music had changed. It had become more dramatic. The strings were still there, hovering in the background, but now the music was all about the piano. Could this really be one man, playing a single piano? No. Not unless he had five hands.

Winston examined the case again. The liner notes included a list of all the musicians. There was only one piano player. Richard Overton. It seemed impossible, but it was true. And even as Winston accepted this, the music amped up yet again, into impossible new heights. Winston found himself wishing he was watching this on television, so he could see this man at work. "Okay, I'm impressed," he said out loud, as if apologizing to Mr. Penrose.

This Overton guy had to be among the greatest musicians ever. If his puzzles and games were half as good as his piano playing, Winston wanted very much to go and see what they were about.

Dinnertime. His father was in a better mood now that the problem at work had been solved. He discussed it with Winston's mom as they served themselves from various dishes on the table. Winston cut into his chicken and waited for a chance to share his news. His blood was pumping with excitement, but he wasn't about to blow this by interrupting his parents.

Winston wondered what sort of games Richard Overton played up there. Would they all have something to do with music? If so, Winston would be sunk. He'd never thought about learning an instrument. He was always buried too deep inside a puzzle book to consider it.

He wondered what it would be like to be able to play the piano. Not like Richard Overton—Winston's imagination had its limits—but well enough to sit down and move his fingers over the keys and hear a melody fill the room. For a moment he could see himself doing it.

But, no. Learning the piano would take hours of hard work. Winston would put off practice because he'd bought a new puzzle book and wanted to start solving, or because he had a new puzzle idea and wanted to put it to paper. Piano would take a backseat to puzzles . . . just like everything else. The thought flashed through his brain that maybe his father was right—that he spent too much time in Puzzle Land.

Well, was that so bad? He really liked solving puzzles. It would kill him to stop. In fact, Winston wondered if it was even *possible* to stop. He'd been doing it for so long that sometimes it felt like the puzzle-solving part of his brain was a separate creature living inside him, one that did nothing but play with words. Just the other day, in the car with his mom, they'd passed a billboard showing an airplane, which for some reason was flying over Mars. Winston had laughed— not at the absurdity of it, but at the unintended wordplay. The two images in the picture were a *planet* and a *plane*: if you took the last letter off the first thing, you got the second. He explained this to his mother, and she gave him a look he was long used to: *I love you, but I sure don't understand you.*

And then that evening—Winston grimaced to remember—he rushed through his homework so that he could create more puzzles like the one he had spotted on the billboard.

The images below can be paired up so that when you remove the final letter from one image, you'll get the other. Can you correctly match up all the pairs?

(Answers, page 242.)

It had been fun presenting the puzzle to his friends that weekend, but his homework had come back spattered with red ink. He had gotten several obvious things wrong. His teacher had written, *I know you know this! Sloppy!* And she had added a frowny face, which was pretty embarrassing.

So maybe he thought about puzzles too much. Maybe. But he still wanted to go to Richard Overton's house.

"And what did you guys do today?" his father asked, as he did almost every day at dinner.

This was the moment. "I visited Mr. Penrose for a while," Winston said. "We played chess."

"Who won?" asked his mother.

"He creamed me," Winston admitted. "But then he got an invitation to a friend's house, and he invited me to go along."

His father looked up from his plate. "You went to Mr. Penrose's friend's house? Where did he live?"

"No, no," Winston corrected. "He only got the invitation today. The party isn't for a couple of weeks. Mr. Penrose has a friend who invites people to his . . ." Winston swallowed back the word *mansion*. "To his house, to play all kinds of puzzle games. Mr. Penrose said I could come along for the weekend. If I wanted."

"For the whole weekend?" asked his mother.

"Yeah. If it's okay. I'd really like to go."

"Well, who is the friend?"

Winston cocked his head, unsure how this next part was going to go. "He's a musician. A piano player. His name is Richard Overton . . . ?"

Forks paused in midair, and his parents stared at him. The silence stretched out long enough that Katie looked around and said, "If he goes away for the weekend, can I go somewhere, too?"

"Richard Overton," said Winston's father. "You know, he's pretty famous." The amusement in Nathan Breen's eyes made it clear this was no small understatement.

Winston nodded. "That's what Mr. Penrose said."

"And you're invited to his house?"

"Yes . . . Can I go?"

His parents looked at each other, dazzled by this unexpected turn of events. "You know," said his father, "when I woke up this morning, I said to myself, I wonder if anybody in this family will ever be invited to the home of a world-famous musician. And now, on this very same day, look what happened."

Katie said, "You really said that?"

"I'm just kidding, sweetie."

Katie rolled her eyes.

"So I can go?" Winston asked. It looked like things were moving in his favor, but he still needed someone to say it.

"I think you can go," said his mother.

"But until then," added his father, "we better not see any notes home from your teachers."

"Okay," said Winston. He'd expected that. He would be walking a tightrope at school for the next two weeks.

"Is he going to play for everyone up there?" asked his father.

"I think he creates the games and we get to play," said Winston.

His father looked at him for a moment and then said, "Is he going to play *the piano*?"

"Oh," said Winston. "I suppose he can if he wants to. It's his house."

His father's smile tightened in a way that Winston understood meant he was trying not to laugh. Well, whatever. Winston had gotten the permission he needed. In his mind he was already running through the carpeted hallways of Richard Overton's estate, looking for a cleverly hidden clue.

"I want to do something fun," said Mal. "Something I can look back on next week when I'm miserable."

"Oh, no," said Jake. "Are you going to complain all day? I'm going home."

"What are you talking about?" Winston said.

Mal said, "What, I didn't tell you?"

They were at their usual table at Rosetti's, another weekend having finally arrived after a long, long school week. Time was playing its usual cruel trick: now that something exciting was on the horizon, the hours had slowed down to an inchworm's crawl. Winston had spent the week drifting through school, trying his best to concentrate on his classwork. There had been other puzzle events in the past, and in the days leading up to them, Winston sank further and further into his daydreams, almost sick with anticipation as the event drew closer. But he couldn't take a two-week mental vacation from school—not ever, and especially not now. Even without a note home from Mr. Burke, if his parents decided that he was goofing off in order to stare at the ceiling and think about Richard Overton's mansion, they would take back their permission in a flash. Winston wasn't about to blow this, so he stayed focused . . . mostly.

At least this weekend he was finally able to get together with his friends.

It was a true October day. Whoever was in charge of the weather had finally realized that it wasn't supposed to be summer anymore.

The afternoon sun was losing a war to an army of smoky gray clouds, and the wind rose and fell in gusts that alarmed the trees. Maybe it would rain, but not for a while, and none of the boys wanted to be indoors. They had biked to their school just to have someplace to go, and played some handball against the playground wall. Then they turned around and headed into town for some pizza.

"What's your news?" Winston asked.

Mal sighed and said, "My sister is graduating high school this year."

Winston squinted at his friend. "That's the news?"

"No. She's looking at colleges next weekend with my parents."

"That's the news?"

"Would you stop asking that? No. This is the news: I have to go with them! They're dragging me all over the state so my sister can look at different dorm rooms."

Jake said, "He actually thought his parents would let him stay at home by himself. Can you believe that? For the whole weekend!"

"Hey," said Mal. "I'm thirteen now!"

"And so mature," Jake said.

Mal grinned and stuffed his mouth with pizza. "Anyway," he said—though it came out *anymumf*—"this coming week I have, like, six different tests, and then next weekend I'm off on the Road Trip of Doom. That's why we have to do something really fun today."

Jake shrugged. "Any suggestions?"

"Horror-movie-athon?" Mal said.

"How many movies are in a 'thon'?" Winston asked.

"I don't know. Seven?"

Jake and Winston hooted at that. "Fourteen hours of watching people get eaten by zombies!" Jake yelled. "Pass."

"Well, you guys come up with something, then."

Something occurred to Winston. "Wait," he said. "It's next week-end that you have to go on this trip?"

"Yeah."

He thought about it some more and then slowly began to smile. "Maybe you can tell your parents that you have other plans."

Jake and Mal stared at him.

They finished their pizza and went down the block to Penrose's shop. Penrose was dusting his shelves with what looked like the entire back half of an ostrich. He seemed pleased when he saw Winston walk in with Jake and Mal.

"Ah, Winston," Penrose said. "I suppose you're not here to play chess. But I'm glad to see you with your friends."

"Yeah, we finally got together. In fact, I have a question about that. Some of these people going to Richard Overton's house, um . . ." Winston searched for a way to ask his question delicately.

Penrose understood immediately. His eyes flicked over to Mal and Jake, who were trying not to look too excited. "You want to ask if some of the guests will have more than one child with them." It looked like Penrose was suppressing a smile. "Yes, I think that will be the case."

"Well, then, I was wondering . . ."

"I think I know what you're wondering," Penrose said. He scratched his chin thoughtfully for a long moment, gazing at the boys, and seemed to make a decision. He said, "I will call my friend Richard and ask him if I might bring a couple more guests. He is a very generous individual, and he will almost certainly say yes." The three friends looked at one another, thrilled and grinning. Penrose continued, "But I want to be clear! I don't want to be your substi-tute father, and I don't want to be put in a position where I have to reprimand you. I was a boy myself once, and I understand what three boys can get up to. I would need you to be on your very best behavior. Do you understand?"

They all spoke at once, trying to make Penrose see how well they understood. "Oh, absolutely!" and "We'll be good!" and "We promise, we totally promise." Penrose, amused, patted the air to quiet them down. He sent them on their way and offered them a puzzle to think about as they left.

"Make it a toughie," Winston said, and Penrose obliged.

What number comes next in this series? (Hint: This is more a word puzzle than a number puzzle!)

1, 4, 3, 11, 15, 13, 17, 24, __

(Answer, page 243.)

THREE

THERE WAS A WHOLE other week to get through. Keeping his mind on classwork was almost impossible. In social studies, Mr. Burke was like a radio station whose signal keeps fading out. Winston was looking at him and watching his lips move, but he had no idea what the teacher was saying. Gripping the edges of his desk, Winston leaned in and tried his best to focus. And he prayed that when Mr. Burke called on somebody, it wouldn't be him.

Mal's parents were skeptical, at first, about his attempt to get out of his sister's college road trip. That was understandable: Mal was a well-established joker, so his parents only laughed when he told them he had been invited to spend the weekend at the mansion of a famous musician. But Mal stuck to his story, and eventually his mother called Penrose and learned that Mal was telling the truth. After some discussion, Mal's parents told him he could go.

For Jake, going to Richard Overton's house meant missing a Saturday swim practice. It was the first time he'd ever skipped out, and the coach had given him a hard time about it. For a couple of days, Winston thought Jake might change his mind. But the temptation of the weekend was too much. Winston felt a little guilty for being so pleased that Jake had chosen his friends over swimming laps in the high school pool.

Somehow, Friday arrived. When the bell rang at the end of eighth period, Winston was first out the door, even though he sat at the opposite end of the classroom. In that one moment, he could have made any sports team in the school. He weaved his way through the crowded hallway, found his locker, retrieved his backpack stuffed with the things he'd need for the weekend, and bolted for the front door.

Outside in the traffic circle was a battered green taxicab. Winston peeked in the window and saw Mr. Penrose sitting in the backseat, reading a newspaper.

"Hey, Mr. Penrose," Winston said.

"Winston!" He folded his paper and got out of the car. "You're ready to go. Good." He opened the trunk. Winston tossed his backpack in, where it sat, dumpy and embarrassed, next to Mr. Penrose's more stylish weekend bag.

Mal was out next, with a bag that was even shabbier than Winston's. "I can hardly believe this," he said, putting his bag in the trunk. "Right now I should be listening to my sister talk for three hours about what sorority she wants to join."

"You owe me big," Winston said, smiling.

"I do!" Mal agreed. "I really do."

Jake exited the school with a camouflage duffel bag, and Mal asked him if he was playing games this weekend or joining the army. Mr. Penrose slid into the front seat next to the cabbie. After a brief tussle over who had to sit in the middle—which Mal lost—the three boys jumped into the back, and they were on their way.

The trip was well over two hours long. Winston told Mr. Penrose that he had listened to Richard Overton's CD and liked it very much, and Mal surprised them all when he said he'd looked up Richard Overton on the Internet, downloaded some of his music, and listened to it all week.

"I never knew I liked classical music," Mal said. "Some of that stuff rocks!"

"It rocks?" Jake teased.

"Well, not *rocks*," Mal said. "You know what I mean."

They talked about school, the boys comparing one of their average days to Mr. Penrose's experiences as a child. Apparently, teachers were once allowed to hit their students, and did so for the slightest reason. Winston was glad he was born after *that* bad idea had faded away.

And of course they talked about puzzles. Winston had come prepared with a few he had thought up, and Mr. Penrose had as well, and they traded little bits of wordplay. Mal and Jake jumped in when they solved something, and even the cabdriver shouted out answers a couple of times.

- **MO___STER.** What two different letters can you put in the blank to make two different common movie bad guys?

- **FINE ARTS.** Can you switch a letter from the first word with a letter from the second word to make a different two-word phrase?

- ___ ___ **CTARI** ___ ___. You can put the same pair of letters in both sets of blanks to make a food. Now can you do it with ___ ___ **MA** ___ ___? How about ___ ___ **I** ___ ___?

- What word becomes its own opposite when you put **FE** in front of it?

- You can add a letter to the word **SCENT**, scramble all the letters, and you'll have another word that means "odor." What is this second word?

- What musical instrument is hiding in the word **COLLECTIVE**?

- What word that means "cold" sounds like a food that's often quite hot?

- What three-letter word meaning "a light touch," when spelled backward, gives you another word meaning "a light touch"?

- Which of the fifty United States contains the word **WHAM**?

(Answers, page 243.)

When they ran out of puzzles, Penrose asked about the boys' families. Both of Mal's parents were teachers, although neither worked in Glenville, which was fine with Mal. "Can you imagine having your dad as a teacher all year?" he asked. "Or even in the same school?" He shuddered theatrically. Jake, when it was his turn, told Penrose that his mother sold real estate and his father worked for a marketing company.

"And that's fun," Jake said, "because he has Adventureland as a client. We got to take a behind-the-scenes tour a few weeks ago."

"Oh, cool," said Winston.

"Yeah, that was fun," said Mal.

Winston said, "Wait . . . you got to go, too?"

There was a slight, uncomfortable pause. "Um, yes?" Mal said.

"Well, where was I?" Winston asked. He tried not to sound

wounded and didn't quite make it. He couldn't believe that Jake would invite Mal but leave him out.

"You were busy that day," Jake said. "I asked you."

Winston had no memory of this. "You asked me if I wanted to go on a private tour of an amusement park, and I said no?"

Jake thought about it. "No. I saw you in the hallway, and I asked what you were doing on Saturday. You said something about an on-line puzzle thing . . . ?"

Winston groaned and slumped over, broken in two by his own stupidity.

"So I didn't even tell you about it," Jake concluded. "I figured you wouldn't be able to go."

"Okay, okay," said Winston, waving at Jake to stop talking. He shook his head and looked out the window. A couple of months back, he'd read about an all-day puzzle contest, to be held over a bunch of different Web sites. That was his kind of thing, of course, so he didn't think twice about signing up. When the day arrived, he was in front of his computer for the noon start time and stayed there for the rest of the day, eating pretzels and solving puzzles. He didn't come close to winning—most of the other contestants were college students and adults—but it was fun, even if Winston was a little bleary-eyed toward the end. Nonetheless, as Winston typed in his final answers and was informed that he'd come in 104th, he glanced out his window at the evening sky and realized he had spent the whole day at his computer. The thought had made him feel a little ill.

And now he'd learned that the puzzle event had cost him a fun time touring Adventureland with his friends, seeing how all the rides worked and who knew what else. It made him feel ill all over again.

"You all right?" Jake asked.

"I'm fine," Winston said. But he wasn't sure he meant it.

They left the highway and traveled through a succession of small towns. A short while later, they turned into a neighborhood where the houses were large and important, each one nestled prettily atop its own sea of lawn. Some had gates blocking the driveway. The trees, all of them stately and majestic, still grasped their multicolored leaves, as if releasing them would disappoint their owners.

The driver made one last turn, onto a curving cobblestone driveway. Up ahead was Richard Overton's house, and yes, it was a mansion. The boys stared, hardly able to take it all in. It was only two stories tall, but it stretched out expansively in either direction from an ornate main entrance. Winston counted more than a dozen windows from left to right on the house's second floor and wasn't sure he had counted them all. The house—the *mansion*—was all brick, with old-fashioned columns here and there adding to the magnificence.

"Whoa," said Winston.

Penrose nodded. "Impressive, isn't it?"

"This guy lives here by himself?" Jake asked.

"He does, yes," Penrose said. "Although his assistant lives in his guesthouse."

"He really lives here all alone?" Mal said. "I guess he can visit a different room every day of the year." The house wasn't *that* big, but Winston knew what he meant.

The battered green taxi looked out of place in front of this castle with its manicured lawn and the sun reflecting a perfect gleam off the polished windows. Winston felt out of place himself. *Impressive* wasn't nearly strong enough a word. This was almost too much.

Would there be a single object in that house Winston could touch without fear of breaking it?

Getting out of the cab, none of them could stop looking up. "I can't believe he got all this by playing the piano," Jake said.

"He plays really well," Mal said.

"I guess he does!"

The cabdriver retrieved their bags from the trunk. Winston looked at his stained and ripped backpack and wanted to hide it in the bushes. He should have borrowed a more grown-up bag from his father.

Penrose paid the cabdriver, then looked at the boys, smiling a bit as he took in their discomfort. He put a gentle hand on Winston's back to guide him up the stone staircase to the front door. "It'll be fine, boys," Penrose said. "This isn't the president of the United States we're visiting."

Jake said, "I think the president has a smaller house."

Penrose laughed. He pushed the doorbell, which chimed merrily.

The door opened a few moments later, and there was Richard Overton. Winston had thought they would be greeted by a servant or his assistant or something, but this was undoubtedly the man himself. He had unruly white hair, and a kind smile on his long, wrinkled face. There was a word to describe what this man brought with him to the front door, and after a moment Winston had it: *stature*. He gave off an aura of importance. Winston thought Richard Overton could wander anywhere in the country, even someplace where nobody had heard of him, and every head would turn while people said to each other, *Who is that? I think that's somebody famous!*

Richard Overton's eyes sparkled, and he exclaimed, "Arthur!" The two men hugged briefly. "I was hoping you'd get here for dinner."

"Of course," said Penrose.

"And these are your boys," said Mr. Overton.

"Well, not *my* boys," said Penrose. "Guests who I think will appreciate your little games." He waved his hand back and forth between the famous musician and the eighth-graders who had come to meet him. "Richard Overton, this is Winston Breen. Richard, don't be surprised if your game runs a little shorter than expected this year. Winston has one of the finest minds for puzzles I have ever encountered."

"Is that right, is that right?" said Richard Overton. He looked at Winston with a curious smile.

Penrose continued, "And these are Winston's friends, with some very sharp minds in their own right. This is Mal, and this is Jake."

"Nice to meet you!" their host said. "Come in, come in." They moved into a large entrance hall. Winston looked around, bowled over by the sight of it all. A chandelier dangled overhead like a million floating diamonds, and to the right a long, extravagant staircase curved around to the second floor. "Just leave your bags here for now," said Richard Overton. "We'll figure out where to put you a little bit later."

From some faraway room, there was a sudden wail: "RYAN HIT ME!" followed by "I DID NOT!" and then the sound of crying. Winston and his friends glanced at one another. Little kids. Winston had hoped all the kids this weekend would be around his own age, but evidently that was not to be.

Richard Overton opted to ignore the screaming. "Norma's in charge of figuring out where everyone will sleep," he said, "and she's a little busy at the moment. I'm not making life easy for her. I gave the staff the weekend off."

Penrose looked surprised. "What? Everybody?"

"I'm sure we can see to ourselves for a few days," said Mr. Overton. "We'll cook food together and clean up together. It'll be the way my old family gatherings used to be."

"Norma is staff, of course," said Penrose. He said to the boys, "She's his assistant. Has been for, what, twenty-five years?"

"About that," agreed Richard Overton. "I think at the twenty-year mark, you're no longer staff, but a family member yourself. Anyway, I'm lost without her—you know that." Indeed, he looked around vaguely for this Norma person to come help these new guests get settled in, but she was nowhere to be seen. "Well, why don't we start with a tour for your young friends?"

Mr. Overton led them through the house—room after gorgeous room. It was like the fanciest hotel Winston could imagine. Every object was perfectly in place and gleamed as if dusted and polished at the top of every hour. There were paintings in the hallways—not prints bought in a store, but real canvases with real oil paint. Winston stared at them like he'd never seen a painting before.

One painting in particular caught Winston's eye. It was abstract— a wild hodgepodge of lines and circles and squares. What made it more interesting was the six other smaller paintings hanging below, done in the same style. Winston's finely honed senses detected a puzzle.

"Ah," said Richard Overton when he saw Winston had been snagged by the paintings. "Do you know Sutton Hammill's work? He makes very playful art. This lovely painting is also a game. Can you find each of the smaller paintings somewhere in the larger one?"

(Answer, page 243.)

After they had stared at the painting awhile, Richard Overton continued the tour, leading them past the fancy staircase and through a pair of glass doors. "The music room, of course." Of course was right. Here was a grand piano the size of a small car, sleek and black and shining. Its top was tilted up, exposing a multitude of hammers and strings.

"Whoa," said Winston when he saw it.

"Really," Jake agreed.

Richard was pleased with their reaction. "I like it when children see the grand piano for the first time," he said to Penrose. "Adults always nod and say 'how lovely,' like they see instruments like this every day. Only children are wise enough to say 'whoa.' Thirty years I've had this piano, and I still say 'whoa' every time I come in here."

"You do?" Mal asked.

Richard smiled. "Well, I say it very quietly."

There were other musical instruments here, too, in a long display case, and in the corner was a cello case, like a soldier permanently saluting. There were two rows of a dozen chairs each, set up in a semicircle. Behind the chairs, a huge wall of windows gave a view to the yard outside.

"We had a little charity event here a couple of nights ago," said Mr. Overton. "We still need to put away the chairs." It was a slight relief to Winston that not everything in this house was in perfect order. Chairs still standing two days after they were needed! Someone get in here and clean up this gigantic mess! Winston suppressed a laugh.

Richard Overton led them through the room to a closed door. He started to open it when a sharp female voice yelled, "No guests in here! Get out!"

Winston jumped back, and even Richard jerked in surprise. He quickly shut the door. "That's right," he said. "We're not allowed in there yet. Sorry."

The door opened up again, and a woman emerged, looking aggravated. She made sure to close the door behind her. "Really, Richard, do you want to ruin everything before it's even begun?"

"You're quite right," Richard said, bowing slightly in deference. "I'd forgotten. Norma, you remember Arthur Penrose . . . ?"

Ah, so this was Norma. She wasn't looking at her boss. She was looking at Winston and Mal and Jake, a frown still etched into her face. She was an older woman with short hair sculpted into place with a series of barrettes, and she peered at the three of them through severe black eyeglass frames.

"More children, then," she said.

"Yes, Norma, I did tell you—"

"I know, I know," she said, waving a hand. "At least these boys are older than the little monsters running around back there."

Richard said to Penrose, "Betty's husband is traveling, and she couldn't find a babysitter. She's always enjoyed my games. I insisted she bring her boys." Back to Norma, he said, "It will be fine. They are no more exuberant than I was at that age."

Norma grunted. "Just keep those children out of here. In fact, keep everyone away." And with that, the woman withdrew into the room. She glared at the boys as she closed the door, as if she suspected them of trying to peek in. Mr. Overton led them away without another word of explanation. The three boys glanced at one another, somewhere between amused and horrified. Richard Overton had kept that chain saw of a woman around for twenty-five years?

The three of them glanced back at the now-closed door. Winston knew they were all thinking the same thing: what is she doing in there?

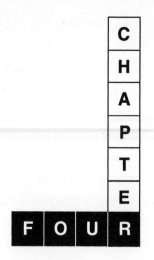

NEXT, THEY WENT into a large, open area off the entrance hall, with many soft couches. This was called the reading room, though there was only a single bookshelf built into the wall, with more doodads and flower vases than books. Winston wondered about that, until Richard said, "Most of the books are downstairs in the library, of course. I bring them up here when I want to get some serious reading done. I'm proud of my library, but this room is sunnier."

So this house had a library. Not a room with a few bookshelves, but a *library*.

"In fact, let's head downstairs," said their host, leading them through the entrance area and down the hall. Winston followed, although not before glancing toward the kitchen, which looked large enough to be used as a helicopter landing pad. This place would never stop being incredible.

They came to a surprisingly long staircase, heading down. Richard navigated the stairs carefully, with both hands on the banister, though he chatted with them the whole time. At the bottom was a hallway—a few doors led to various rooms, and then the passage opened up to what was clearly the library. Winston began walking toward it, but their host turned the other way, and Winston had to reverse course. At the other end of the hall was a closed door. Richard opened it to reveal a dark room with some sort of light flickering inside it.

"Oh," said Richard. "Someone is using the theater."

"The theater?" Jake said. "Like, a movie theater?" They all poked their heads inside, and sure enough, it was a genuine movie theater. The light bouncing off the screen was enough to illuminate two short rows of plush red seats.

"Chase, is that you in there?" Richard called out.

"Yes, is that okay?" The image on the screen froze, and Chase came to the door, squinting because of the light in the hallway.

Mr. Overton assured Chase that it was fine to use the theater, while Winston stared at this new guest. Chase was a rugged-looking middle-aged man in crisp blue jeans and a sporty shirt. Every black hair on his head was perfectly in place, though he also sported a three-day growth of stubble. He looked very, very familiar.

"Chase, you remember Arthur Penrose."

"Of course," said Chase, and the two men shook hands.

"And these are Arthur's friends." Richard waved a finger at the boys as if trying to remember their names. "This is Winston, and Mal, and Jake."

Chase smiled and stuck out his hand. "Chase Worthington. Nice to meetcha." Winston's own hand went out on autopilot, while his mouth opened in surprise yet again. Chase smiled the smile of someone used to being recognized. Chase Worthington was an actor. He had his own television show . . . something about a lawyer helping people for free. Winston had never seen it, but he knew this man was very famous.

"Is Zook in there with you?" Richard asked.

Winston thought, Zook? What's a Zook?

Chase shook his head. "Watch a movie with his *father*? Perish the thought. I think he's in the pool. I hope that's okay."

"It's fine," Richard assured him again, and from off in the distance they heard the doorbell ring. "Oh!" said their host, jumping slightly. "Another arrival." He creaked his way up the stairs while Winston's head twisted back and forth, looking longingly at the theater he hadn't quite seen and the library he hadn't gotten to see at all.

Back in the entrance hall, Richard opened the door. Three new arrivals entered. First in was a very tall, broad-shouldered man wearing a three-piece suit, like he had just come from a board meeting. He was carrying about five bags at once. Behind him was a woman, heavily made up and with a carefully shaped helmet of hair on her head. Then came a girl a little older than Winston, wearing a simple but pretty blue-and-white dress. She dropped her surprisingly large suitcase, then crossed her arms like she had just lost an argument. She was certainly *not* looking around this magnificent palace with wonder in her eyes.

Richard greeted the man and his wife with a brief embrace, then shook the girl's hand. The girl was unsmiling and wouldn't look Mr. Overton in the eye. The wife then whispered something to Mr. Overton, who pointed down the hall. She danced off, obviously in need of a bathroom.

"That guy looks familiar," Jake said quietly.

"I was thinking the same thing," said Mal. "Another actor?"

Richard Overton asked if they had a good flight, and the man laughed. "We drove! We made it into a family road trip. Didn't we,

Amanda?" Amanda's face was a perfect neutral mask. Her father stared at her for a moment and then continued. "We stopped at forty EZ Burgers on the way. That's why we didn't fly. I wanted to drop in on my restaurants. Just a man and his wife and daughter stopping in for a meal. I wasn't recognized once, was I, honey?"

Amanda sighed. "No," she said. "Not once."

The boys' eyes widened, and Winston glanced up at Mr. Penrose, who nodded in answer to the unasked question: this was Gerard Deburgh, the man who owned the entire chain of EZ Burger restaurants. Incredible. Was there anybody Richard Overton didn't know? Winston wouldn't be surprised if the next guy to walk in was the king of Portugal. Assuming Portugal had a king.

"This last leg was a solid five hours, and we had to floor it a little to make decent time. That's why Candice there had to run off." He laughed again, then said, "And to keep Amanda from going crazy, I promised her some of Vera's homemade sorbet. Is that all right?"

Richard said, "Vera's not here, I'm afraid."

Gerard looked alarmed. "Is she okay?"

"She's fine. I sent her away. I sent all the help away for the weekend."

"What?" Gerard was astounded. "What are we going to eat?"

"Vera's done plenty of shopping. We have all the food we'll need. We just have to cook it."

Gerard looked dubious, but tried on a smile and said, "Well, you're the host. I'm sure it's going to be a great weekend. Right, Amanda? And look! Kids your age."

Amanda, looking at the three boys, said her longest string of words thus far: "They're not my age. They're younger."

There was a brief, poisonous silence before Mal responded. "That's true," he said. "I'm only five years old."

Gerard laughed, ignoring the chill that had developed between his daughter and the boys. "Arthur," he said to Mr. Penrose, "it's good to see you again. Are these your grandchildren?"

"No," said Penrose. "Just friends." He placed a hand on each of their shoulders in turn: "This is Winston, Mal, and Jake."

"Nice to meet you all!" said Gerard, with a forced merriment. He glanced over to Amanda, waiting for her to join the fun. Winston thought he'd be waiting a long time.

Jake said, "We should have asked for some bread crumbs to leave behind us, so we can find our way back to the kitchen."

"Probably any bread crumbs you drop are cleaned up immediately," Winston said.

Mal laughed. "Oh, you know this guy has one of those robot vacuum cleaners. Drop something on the floor, and—*voom!*—this thing on wheels shoots out to get it. Drop something else on the floor, and the robot picks *you* up and drags you outside."

They'd been given the run of the house while the adults cooked dinner. Gerard Deburgh tried to get Amanda to go along with them—"Go! Explore the house with your new friends!"—but Amanda said with wooden politeness, "No, thanks," and walked away. This was fine with Winston.

Jake wanted to get a better look at the movie theater, and Winston wanted to see the library, so they started off downstairs. As they neared the theater, they heard the raucous sound of kids screeching at each other. Jake peeked in and was surprised to find all the lights on. There was no movie playing. Instead, two young boys were having an endless chase around the rows of seats, screaming nonstop while they ran.

"Oh, I'm sorry," said a voice. A woman stood up, looking worried. "Did you want to watch a movie?"

"No, no, that's okay," said Jake.

"Because I can take my kids outside—Ryan! Ian!" she suddenly exploded. "Be quiet! Mommy's talking!" Ryan and Ian paused to look at her, and then continued running and screaming as if nothing had happened.

Their mother shrugged and shook her head: *What can you possibly do?* "Anyway," she said, "I'm Betty McGinley. Nice to meet you."

Winston, Mal, and Jake introduced themselves, and they tried to have a conversation, but it was impossible—her kids were like a pair of broken car alarms. They got out of there as fast as they could.

"Holy smoke," Mal said when they had shut the theater door, which muted but did not eliminate the screaming from inside. "I'm sure looking forward to hanging out with *them* all weekend."

Jake said as they walked down the hallway, "Richard Overton invited them, but now he's gotta be saying, I should have set an age limit."

Winston agreed. "No one under ten years old."

Mal added, "Or over a hundred decibels!"

At that moment, a sound that must have been a *thousand* decibels came blasting out of one of the other rooms—a chord from an electric guitar. The volume lowered immediately, as if someone had put on music without realizing how loud the stereo was set. The boys opened a door and peeked into what turned out to be an entertainment room. There were a couple of comfortable sofas aimed at a small television and a truly amazing amount of stereo equipment, with speakers almost as tall as Winston himself. A waist-high book-case ran the length of the room, filled with CDs and record albums. The top of these shelves was littered with awards and plaques and statuettes.

Standing at the stereo was a boy, fifteen or sixteen years old, with a mess of long wavy hair, in a T-shirt and ripped jeans. He was tall—Winston's mother would have called him "gangly"—with a long face like an upside-down triangle. He looked up, frowning, as the boys came in.

He turned off the stereo and said bluntly, "I have this room."

Winston was taken aback. "We're just looking around."

"Look around somewhere else." He continued to examine the stereo.

The three boys looked at one another, shrugged, and backed out of the room. Winston was gladder than ever that Mal and Jake were here. Imagine being stuck for the weekend with cold-as-ice Amanda, those bratty brothers, and now this morose thug of a teenager.

"That must be Zook," Jake said as they exited the room.

Mal said, "He's probably angry about his name."

They glanced into a bathroom and two offices along the hall. On what must have been Richard Overton's desk, Winston noticed a small stack of puzzle magazines. He smiled; it was like friends had followed him here. Maybe he would ask to borrow one later if things got boring.

A second later he rolled his eyes, annoyed with himself for even having that thought. Was that how he wanted to spend his time here? Curled up in a room with the same puzzle magazine he could work on at home? Seriously, what was wrong with him?

As they approached the library, Winston could see that it was amazing—a magnificent cavern of books, with dark wood flooring and shelves from floor to ceiling, going on forever. There were even a couple of those rolling ladders to help you get stuff from high places. Winston couldn't wait to get in there and explore.

But, once again, no. As they neared the library, a voice called from upstairs. "Kids? Are you down there? We need a couple more hands up here! Come on up and help set the table!" The three boys froze and looked at one another. Well, heck.

"Hello?" came that voice again. "Anybody down there?"

"We're coming!" yelled Jake, and the three boys, a bit frustrated, headed back to the stairs.

"Wait a sec," said Mal as they passed the stereo room. He knocked and opened the door without waiting for a reply. Zook looked up sharply. "They want us upstairs," Mal said. "We gotta help with dinner." He shut the door again as Zook glowered.

As they walked up the stairs, Mal said, "We're *all* supposed to help with dinner, right?"

"Oh, absolutely," Jake and Winston agreed.

Dinner was spectacular. The table looked like something out of a story with lots of kings and princesses. Food was laid out from end to end—a platter of juicy chicken cutlets, a thinly sliced steak, baskets of biscuits, bowls of vegetables and grains and side dishes, only some of which Winston recognized. The plates and glasses and silverware had the same expensive shine as everything else in the house, and five elegant candles burned at various points along the table.

Winston had feared he would be stuck at a kids' table, but that had been reserved only for Ryan and Ian, whose hands and faces were already a mess. Everyone else was seated at the large dining room table. There were fifteen of them, which was a little crowded even for a table this long, but they made do without elbowing one another too much.

Winston assumed he'd be sitting next to his friends, or perhaps Penrose, but Richard Overton had other ideas. He'd pointed them to various seats as they walked in, sometimes changing his mind and forcing someone who was already seated to stand up and move somewhere else. By the time he was done, nobody was sitting next to anybody they had arrived with.

Winston was seated next to a short man, neat and polished in a brown suit and bow tie, with curly, graying hair. He had a darker complexion—South American, maybe—but spoke with a slight English accent. He introduced himself as Derek Bibb, and across the table, Mal looked thunderstruck.

"Derek Bibb?" Mal asked. "Did you say you're Derek Bibb?"

"Yes. Hello. Call me Derek."

Whoever Derek Bibb was, his presence seemed to have short-circuited Mal's brain. He gawked at Winston's neighbor, jaw slightly unhinged. Derek Bibb smiled as if this was not the first time he had experienced this.

On Winston's other side was a woman beautiful enough to be on magazine covers. Indeed, with her rich blond hair and her shiny red dress, she might have come here directly from a photo shoot. Winston tried not to stare, but his head kept turning that way on its own, like a compass needle to magnetic north. She introduced herself to him, with a dazzling smile, as Kimberly Schmidt. Winston, positive he must be turning red, nodded a hello and shook her soft hand and perhaps even croaked out his own name.

He looked around and saw Jake sitting next to Richard Overton, near the head of the table. Richard at this moment stood up and clinked his glass with his fork until the hum of conversation died down. Behind him at the kids' table, even Ryan and Ian stopped yelling at each other for a few moments.

Richard thanked everybody for coming, old friends and new friends alike, and promised he would not make a long speech that would cause all this delicious food to grow cold.

"Especially since there were no appetizers and everyone is starving," interrupted Norma with a grumble.

"No one is starving," Richard said patiently.

"I could have sworn Vera told me she'd bought them," Norma said. "I'll be having words with her, you can be sure of that. There were supposed to be stuffed mushrooms and lamb meatballs. Right before she left, I asked her—"

"Anyway!" Richard said, earning a scowl from Norma. From the way the two of them acted, Winston might have guessed that Norma was the boss of Richard instead of the other way around.

Their host continued. "I just wanted to welcome you all, and I hope you have a wonderful weekend full of puzzles and games and friendship. Now let's eat."

The meal was fantastic, one of the best of Winston's life. Between forkfuls of salad, Richard Overton demanded updates on everybody's life, and Winston listened to the stories with astonished ears.

Over there, large as life, was Lawrence Rossdale, the boyish and pink-cheeked weatherman from the daytime talk show *Good Morning!* Winston never watched it, but you'd have to live in a cave not to know the man. Rossdale—"Call me Larry! I'm only Lawrence on television!"—had turned his relentless cheerfulness at the weather map into a career endorsing dozens of products in various TV commercials. Even now, Winston half expected him to hold up a bottle of steak sauce and start talking about it.

Instead he told the group how he had just sold a line of books to a publisher—"weather-related mysteries," he called them. "The first one is going to be called *Storm Front*, and then *Heat Wave*. You see?" Larry looked happily around, and everyone nodded with approval.

Derek Bibb, Winston's neighbor at the table, talked about the play he was getting ready to launch on Broadway. Broadway! Even Winston knew to be impressed at that. So Derek Bibb was a theater director. That explained Mal's reaction. Winston hadn't realized Mal followed theater so closely.

Derek talked about his play the way Winston's English teacher went on about certain books, discussing the plot, the characters, the theme, and heaven knows what else. He actually stood up at the table like he'd been hired to give a lecture. His audience was all smiles to start, but one by one, those smiles faded—Derek seemed ready to talk about this play all night. Richard finally had to interrupt him so they could continue their way around the table. Derek blinked like a man coming out of a hypnotic trance, and then gave a surprised little laugh. "I lose my mind a little when I'm on a new production," he said. "My apologies." He waved a hand, indicating he was finished, and sat back down.

"Nothing wrong with being excited about a project," Richard said.

"But we don't want to be sitting here all night, either," Gerard added, to some amiable laughter.

Winston's other neighbor, Kimberly Schmidt, was neither an actress nor a model—she was a musician. In fact, that was her cello standing upright in the music room. She told everyone that the following week she would be flying to Australia to play at the Sydney Opera House, which earned some oohs and aahs.

The TV actor Chase Worthington talked about whether or not his show would be picked up for another season. "It could go either way.

But I'm glad for this hiatus, so I can spend some more time with my son." He smiled a toothy, professional actor's smile at Zook, who didn't look up from his meal.

It turned out that Betty McGinley was a radio deejay, and she had a lovely, melodic voice when she wasn't screaming at her kids. She told a funny story about hosting an awards banquet. Apparently a very famous person had fallen off the stage and into a three-tiered cake.

When it was Gerard Deburgh's turn to speak, he briefly mentioned opening another five EZ Burgers and then turned the spotlight on his family. "Candice here," he said, gesturing to his wife, "has opened up a lovely antiques shop just a few miles from where we live. She has quite an eye for art and antiques." Candice nodded, smiling, in full agreement with her husband. "And as for Amanda," Gerard continued, "she is only going to be the next Richard Overton. Count on it."

Amanda was looking down at her plate, studying her food with great interest.

"Oh, you play piano?" asked Kimberly Schmidt.

"Yes," Amanda said quietly.

"You'll have to play for us at some point this weekend," said Larry Rossdale.

"Of course she will!" said her father, beaming.

Amanda looked up and attempted a smile, but mostly she looked like she wanted to crawl under the table. Winston wondered if maybe her father was overstating things a little. He guessed that Amanda was probably pretty good, but was she really the next Richard Overton? That was a lot to live up to.

Richard, sensing that Amanda had had enough attention, turned to Penrose. "Any travels to report, Arthur?"

Winston had wondered what Penrose would say to match these

incredible stories. It turned out that twice a year, Penrose took trips to different places throughout the world. Winston had no idea that when the CLOSED sign appeared on Penrose's shop, it meant Penrose had flown off to Ecuador, or China, or Madagascar.

"Six weeks from now, I'm heading back to Paris," said Penrose. "Haven't been there in forty years." That led to a whole conversation about the things he should see and do there, and the restaurants he should eat in and avoid. Mal and Jake and Winston kept trading disbelieving, wondering smiles. Usually on a Friday evening, if they could get together at all, the three of them would sit around playing board games or watching a movie. This was a whole other kind of experience.

"And what about our younger guests?" Richard Overton said, looking around. "What do you have to say for yourselves?" He turned to his left. "Jake, is it? What are your interests?"

Jake looked surprised to find himself in the spotlight. He must have assumed—as Winston had—that only the grown-ups would be speaking, bragging about their accomplishments. Jake glanced around, and Winston knew what he was thinking: what can I say that could compare with these people?

"Well, I like sports," he said. "I'm swimming now. In the spring I'll be back on the baseball team."

"What position?" Richard Overton asked.

"Third base."

"The hot corner!" Larry Rossdale said, waving his fork in Jake's direction. "Well done! No team worth its salt puts anybody at third who isn't a real athlete."

Jake smiled, pleased.

Their host turned next to Zook Worthington, who stared off at an imaginary point on the far wall, like he was trying to pretend he wasn't here. Winston didn't think he would even respond, but Zook shrugged and said, "I'm just doing stuff," he said. "You know. Whatever."

A disappointed silence greeted this. Zook looked around briefly to see his father frowning and rubbing his forehead. Zook ducked his head and went back to his food.

Richard, seeing he wasn't going to get anything else from Zook, continued his way around the table. "Amanda we have already heard from—our future maestro. How about you, young man? Remind me of your name, please."

"Mal," said Mal. "And I want to be an actor. You know, someday. Not now. Although I'm in my school play now." Winston had never seen Mal this nervous. He kept looking and then trying not to look at Derek Bibb, who was smiling with encouragement. "Anyway, that's what I'm doing," Mal concluded, his face bright red.

"What play are you in?" Derek Bibb asked.

"What play?" Mal repeated. He blinked. His mind had gone as blank as an empty road. "Uh," he said. "Oh! *Arsenic and Old Lace.*"

Derek Bibb gave a satisfied nod. "A classic indeed."

"Yes. Yes. A classic," Mal agreed, and turned to look at Richard Overton as if to say, I would like to be done talking now.

Richard took the hint. Winston knew he was next, and he was right. "How about you, Winston?" Richard looked around the table and said, "Arthur tells me Winston knows everything there is to know about puzzles."

"Is that right?" asked Larry Rossdale. "You've certainly come to the right place this weekend."

"No fair outshining the grown-ups, though," said Kimberly Schmidt, waving a kidding finger at him. Winston responded with a grin that he hoped wasn't too foolish.

"What do you intend to do with it?" asked Gerard Deburgh.

Winston blinked at him. "Do with what?"

"Do with the puzzles . . . not much money in that, is there?"

"The boy is twelve," said Mr. Penrose, a bit scornfully. "It's a hobby and a passion. He doesn't have to worry about whether or not it will support his life."

Gerard shrugged, not as if he agreed but as if it would be impolite to argue at the dinner table.

"So give us a puzzle, then," said Derek Bibb, wiping his lips with his cloth napkin.

"If you have anything prepared," said Richard.

Penrose chuckled. "He's always prepared," he said. "And if he's not, he'll create something on the spot. I've seen it. Many times."

All eyes were on Winston now, which was a little intimidating, but the fact was, he *did* have a puzzle idea. On the sideboard behind him was a little cylinder filled with toothpicks. He reached for it and spread some toothpicks out on the table.

"This is sort of a classic puzzle," Winston said. "Can you move three toothpicks and make three squares of the same size, and have no toothpicks left over?"

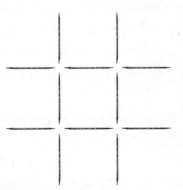

(Answer, page 244.)

52

AFTER DINNER THE ADULTS sat around talking, and the kids were allowed to do as they pleased, so Winston and his friends went outside. They weren't out for very long—the sun had just about set, and they soon felt like a trio of cat burglars creeping across the lawn. Still, what they saw was impressive. A winding brick path connected the main house to the guesthouse where Norma lived. It was smaller but no less fancy. Off to the side but between the two houses was an elaborate garden, and near that was a shed almost as large as Winston's garage. Mal wanted to peek inside, but Jake pointed out that the doors were padlocked shut.

On the side of the house, they encountered a long patio floored with bricks of varying pale colors. There was furniture back here, and what was probably a grill, but each object had been covered with a tarp. Mal found a switch and flicked it, and a row of small spotlights illuminated the whole area.

"I can't get over this place," Winston said, looking around. From this point, he couldn't even see to the end of the property, and there was certainly no sign of neighbors. "How many concerts do you think he had to perform to buy this house?"

"Maybe one," said Mal, "and they paid him a billion dollars."

Jake called to them. "Hey! Look at this."

He was looking at the ground at a particular bunch of bricks, all of them engraved with numbers. Winston wasn't sure what it meant until Jake pointed to a small metal sign, which informed them this was . . . a maze! Built right into the patio!

"Wow," Mal said. "You know Winston's going to have a maze in his backyard when he's older."

"No," said Winston. "My entire house is going to be a maze."

Starting from the circled 4 in the upper left corner, travel in a straight line along the rows and columns (no diagonals!) until you reach the F in the lower right. The space you are currently on tells you how many spaces you must move—so you'll start by jumping 4 squares either across or down, and that will give you a new number for your next move. Can you reach the finish?

4	4	4	3	5	2
3	2	2	4	4	3
3	1	2	2	4	5
5	3	3	2	4	5
3	1	4	1	1	3
2	2	3	4	5	F

(Answer, page 244.)

It was a big house, but it didn't have an infinite number of bedrooms, and there were a lot of guests. Richard suggested that there were plenty of sofas scattered around, and the kids could sleep on these. Amanda's face darkened at this suggestion. She whispered something in her mother's ear, and before you knew it, she had a bedroom of her own. Winston thought that was pretty unfair, but then it turned out that Betty McGinley had offered to sleep in the guesthouse with her two kids (who were still running around—would they never get tired?). Winston could sense a feeling of relief that Ryan and Ian wouldn't be screaming in the main house all night—so all in all, everything worked out.

Zook was pointed to the entertainment room in the basement, where Winston had first encountered him. As for Winston and Jake and Mal, they were all put together in the large reading room near the entrance hall, each on his own cushy sofa. Norma provided them with pillows, sheets, and blankets. Kimberly, somewhat shyly, requested an extra-warm blanket she had used last time, but they weren't able to find it. It wasn't in the downstairs closet where it was supposed to be, which irritated Norma, who obviously felt it was her job to get every detail of this weekend perfect. Kimberly rushed to assure her that she would be just as happy with any blanket.

The boys took their bedding to the reading room and set to work building their little nests. The day had been a long one. Had Winston really been sitting in a boring school classroom earlier today?

Winston's sofa was comfortable but unfamiliar, and he woke up a few times during the night. And then, as daylight started coming through the windows, Norma's keys rattled in the front door, jarring him awake yet again. She marched down the hall to the kitchen and could soon be heard banging around pots and pans. She must not have been very pleased with her boss's decision to let the other help go for the weekend.

Despite the noise, Winston dozed off again. By the time he woke up for good, his pillow had fallen to the floor and the bedsheet had rumpled up beneath him. He sat up, groggy-eyed. Mal was out cold, but Jake was up and gone.

Winston had slept in a pair of sweatpants, and to this he added a T-shirt. Sounds were coming from the kitchen and dining room, so he padded over to see what was happening.

Most of the bustle was coming from the kitchen, but Winston passed through the dining room to get there. The table was once again laid out with a fantastic array of foods, and at that moment, Norma came in from the kitchen to add more to it—a plate of waffles.

"Good morning," she said, somehow making even this sound abrupt. "Breakfast will be ready in a few minutes. Please wait elsewhere while I finish setting up."

"Sure," Winston said, easing himself past her and into the kitchen. Most of the grown-ups were drinking coffee. Penrose and Jake were both fully dressed and chatting. Winston joined them, rubbing the last of the grogginess out of his eyes.

"Did you see the table?" Jake asked.

"The dining room table?" Winston said. "Sure." He thought that was a strange question, considering Jake had just watched Winston walk in from the dining room.

Jake leaned in. "So what do you think?"

"It's a lot of food," Winston said.

Penrose, smiling, said to Jake, "I think he didn't notice. You just woke up, didn't you, Winston?"

"Yeah," Winston said, gesturing to his sweatpants and T-shirt. "What didn't I notice?"

"Maybe nothing," Penrose said. "We'll see. I think breakfast is about to be served." He gestured with his chin back to the dining room entrance, where Richard Overton stood, hands on hips, studying the table. He muttered something to Norma, who made some minute adjustments to the food. Satisfied, Richard turned around and announced into the kitchen, "Good morning, friends! Breakfast is ready."

The guests paraded in, some dressed for the day and others still in sleepwear and bathrobes. Mal came in from the reading room, his hair disheveled and his eyes glued shut with sleep.

"Guh," he said, and turned around and left again, sparking some laughter among the more awake.

"Please pass the yogurt?" asked Kimberly Schmidt, pointing to the opposite end of the table. There was a large bowl with an assortment of yogurts embedded in a rockpile of crushed ice.

"Of course," said Candice Deburgh. She picked up the bowl and started to pass it down.

Norma was there in an instant. "Leave the bowl where it is, please."

Candice froze, unexpectedly chastised. She placed the bowl down gently, looking confused.

Norma said to Kimberly, "What flavor do you want?"

"Um . . . strawberry?"

Norma plucked a strawberry yogurt out of the bowl and walked it over to the musician. "Please leave the foods on the table where I've placed them," she announced to the group.

Jake nudged Winston. "You see?"

"See? See what?"

Jake whispered, "This is a puzzle!"

Winston was bewildered. "What is?"

Jake gestured at the whole table, and for the first time, Winston saw it. The foods had been laid out in distinct groups of three. At the far end was a platter of assorted cheeses, a plate of what looked like sausage links, and a silver mesh bowl holding packets of oatmeal. Partway down the table was the next set: a pitcher of cold milk, a plate of bagels, and the rapidly disappearing stack of waffles. The third set consisted of three bowls, one containing hard-boiled eggs, another with fresh oranges, and a third with something creamy and yellow. Vanilla pudding? That was a strange breakfast choice, although since it was here, Winston decided to help himself to some of it.

There were two more groupings of food on the table. A plate of bacon sat next to a plate of toast and a bowlful of red and green apples. And finally there was the yogurt, next to a number of grapefruit, which in turn were next to a bowlful of raisins.

Jake was right. This was a strange array of foods, and the fact that they were grouped into sets of three made it stranger still. And Norma seemed absolutely determined that nobody should move anything. This had to be the first puzzle.

Across from Winston, Derek Bibb was looking this way and that along the table, a spoonful of oatmeal paused en route to his mouth. Derek and Winston caught each other's eye, and Derek suppressed a smile. So Derek knew, too, that there was something odd going on.

Most people, however, didn't. Food was grabbed up, and occasionally Norma or Richard Overton would step in to adjust a plate, though only Norma would bark at someone who was trying to pass food down the table. Gerard Deburgh, a pair of waffles on his own plate, asked where the syrup was. Norma said it was in the kitchen, on the counter.

Gerard harrumphed as he stood up. "Why not keep it on the table? Next to the waffles, maybe?"

"Because we kept it in the kitchen," said Richard. "Please leave it there."

Shaking his head at his host's quirkiness, Gerard left the room with his plate.

Other houseguests wandered in. Chase Worthington looked as professionally handsome as ever, and had even shaved off his stubble. His son looked like he had just fallen out of bed. Zook was wearing the same clothes as yesterday, and his long hair kept wanting to make a curtain in front of his face.

"Good morning, everybody!" Chase said, while Zook took an empty plate and began examining his choices for breakfast.

At the head of the table was Larry Rossdale. As Winston watched, Larry slowly stood up. He looked across the table like the food had started talking to him. He glanced up at Richard, who was watching this with a sly smile.

"So when do the games start?" Larry asked with suspicion.

"What makes you think they haven't started already?" Richard answered.

That stopped everybody. "What?" asked Kimberly. "We're playing a game?"

"The food is a puzzle," Larry said. "I *thought* something was going on here. So what's the deal?"

"That's what you have to figure out," said Richard.

"I notice the food has been placed into particular sets," said Derek. "Sets of three."

"Aha," said Richard, beaming. "I've been waiting for someone to make that observation. I'll tell you this much: each set of food has something in common. Once you figure that out, it's a simple jump to this puzzle's answer." And with that, Richard pulled out a chair and sat, smiling at his guests like a kid amused by a cage full of hamsters.

Everybody stopped eating, and a dozen pairs of eyes flitted around the table, as the guests tried to make sense of what they'd just been told.

"Oatmeal and cheese have something in common?" asked Kimberly.

Richard only smiled more broadly and shrugged.

"They're both vegetarian dishes," Chase observed.

"And they're sitting next to a plate of sausages," said Kimberly.

"Oh. Right."

Winston had all but forgotten the food on his own plate. Raisins and grapefruit were both fruit. Right? Were raisins considered a fruit? Even if they were, what did that have to do with yogurt?

"Should we be working on this together?" asked Penrose. "Or should we be working individually?"

Richard said, "You may feel free to share ideas if you'd like. Only one person will win the prize, however."

"Prize? There's a prize?" asked Chase.

"A very nice prize," Richard said.

Ryan and Ian—Winston had started to think of them together as the brats—ran into the room with their usual high degree of chaos, followed by their mother. "I'll just feed them in the kitchen, if that's okay," said Betty McGinley. That was perfectly fine with everybody, although when she tried to take the plate of waffles off the table to give to her kids, Norma was there in a flash to stop her.

Looking around at the food, Kimberly said, "I keep wanting to say these are all things people eat for breakfast."

"I think the answer is going to be more specific than that," said

Derek. He had taken out a little notepad and was writing things down.

Winston thought that was a very good idea. He ran to the reading room and rooted through his knapsack until he found a notebook and a pen. As he came back into the dining room, Candice Deburgh said, "Are you sure these groups have been properly arranged?"

"Quite sure," Richard said.

"So you're saying that bacon and apples have something in common?" She shook her head, baffled at the idea of it.

Her daughter, Amanda, remained aloof from the whole situation, calmly sitting at a corner of the table eating a yogurt.

Winston sat back down next to Jake and Mr. Penrose and got busy writing.

"What do you think?" Jake said in a low voice.

"I think staring at the food isn't going to get us anywhere," Winston said, and Penrose nodded in agreement.

Winston wrote down words, and soon the three of them were looking at the page intently.

OATMEAL	MILK	EGGS
CHEESE	BAGELS	ORANGES
SAUSAGE	WAFFLES	PUDDING

BACON	YOGURT
TOAST	GRAPEFRUIT
APPLES	RAISINS

(Continue reading to see the answer to this puzzle.)

"Well, BACON and TOAST and APPLE all have five letters," said Jake.

"I suppose," said Winston. "Except it's not just one apple. Right? That's why I wrote APPLES, as a plural."

"Besides that," said Penrose, "that idea doesn't seem to work for any other group."

"Wait a minute," said Winston. He was still thinking of these things as *foods*. But Jake was surely right—the answer would have something to do with the words themselves. Maybe not the number of letters in each one, but *something* along those lines.

And, boom, he saw what it had to be. His finger traced down each short column, and his idea was confirmed as he went along. "I have it," he whispered excitedly.

"You do? Really?" Jake leaned in.

Winston squinted at his paper. "I have everything but an actual answer," he said. Then, almost immediately, the rest of the answer slid neatly into place. He stood up breathlessly.

"The answer is LARGE," he said to Richard, nearly shouting in his excitement.

Richard shook his head. "No."

"No?" Winston couldn't believe it. He looked down at his paper. The answer had to be an anagram of those letters. "Then the answer is REGAL," he said.

"Sorry," said their host.

"Um, Winston . . . ," said Penrose, patting Winston on the shoulder in an attempt to make him sit down. Winston barely noticed. He was studying his notebook furiously.

"Where are you getting this from?" Larry asked.

"I don't get it either," said Kimberly.

Incredibly, it was Amanda Deburgh who spoke up next. Winston had dismissed her entirely. She'd been dragged here by her parents— it was clear that she had no interest in Richard Overton's games. But now she announced, "The answer is ELGAR."

"Exactly so!" Richard clapped his hands together with joy.

"ELGAR?" Winston said. "What sort of word is ELGAR?"

"He's a composer," said Amanda. "Everybody knows that."

"Don't be rude, Amanda," said her mother. "Obviously *not* everybody knows that."

"Whatever. Do I win?"

"You do indeed!" said Richard. "Well done."

"Wait a minute, wait a minute," said Chase, standing up. "How did we get from a bunch of breakfast foods to Edward Elgar?" He scanned the table for the signs that had eluded him. Next to him, Zook kept on eating.

"Would you like to explain, Amanda?" Richard asked her.

Amanda shrugged. "This kid," she said, nodding her head at Winston, "thought the answer was LARGE or REGAL. I figured if the answer had those letters in it, it might be a famous composer like ELGAR. So I guessed that."

Winston turned to Jake, his jaw open in disbelief. She hadn't solved the puzzle at all! She just rode in on Winston's back and snatched the answer away! And she called him a *kid*! She couldn't be more than a year or two older.

"But how did you get those letters in the first place?" Chase asked. He, anyway, was looking at Winston and not Amanda when he asked this question.

"In each group, the three foods have something in common," Winston said. "It turns out, the three foods all share exactly one letter."

He pointed to the oatmeal, cheese, and sausage. "All three of those foods have a letter E. The next group shares an L, and then it's G, A, and R."

"So you solved it," said Derek, "but you didn't realize those letters spelled something."

Winston nodded, trying not to seem upset about it. "I thought I had to anagram them into a word. That's why I said LARGE and REGAL."

"Well!" Gerard beamed around the table, trying to get the attention back over to his daughter. "Good job, Amanda! First puzzle out, and you've already won a prize. How about that?"

"Cool," Amanda said. "What'd I win?"

Richard paused before answering, and Winston thought maybe he was deciding who should really be the winner of this puzzle. Then he said to Amanda, "You'll see what you've won in just a few minutes." Turning to Winston, he said, "I'm sorry, Winston. You didn't say the right answer. I applaud you for finding the right path, however. Well done." He stood up and announced to the group, "Please finish eating, and let's gather in the reading room. Good morning, all of you!" He left the room, followed by Norma.

"Sorry," Penrose said to Winston. "That was very nice solving. Too bad you got led astray."

"That's all right, I guess." He was still a little stunned. This must be how a football quarterback feels when a perfectly thrown pass is intercepted by the other team. "If all the answers this weekend are different composers, I am toast."

"Me too," said Jake.

"Nonsense," said Penrose. "We'll work together, and I'll fill in any gaps in your knowledge. I was trying to do that a minute ago. Like

Amanda, I thought the answer might be ELGAR, but I was trying to whisper it to you so you could claim it for yourself."

"Oh, rats," said Winston. "You were?" Belatedly, he remembered Penrose's hand on his shoulder. He'd been trying to tell him something. Winston sighed. "Next time I'll listen."

Mal ventured into the dining room, looking much more awake. He had showered and dressed. "Hey," he said to everybody, "did I miss breakfast?"

"I CAN'T BELIEVE I missed the first puzzle," Mal said. "Why didn't someone get me?"

"I assumed you were coming right back," said Jake. "And then we got into the puzzle and just . . ."

"Forgot," Winston said.

"That's great," said Mal sourly. "At least they didn't clear away the food after the puzzle was solved. So what was it?"

"What was what?" Winston said.

Mal was exasperated. "What was the *puzzle*? What did I miss?"

"Oh." They explained it to him, and Winston showed him his notepad. "See? The answer was ELGAR."

"Elgar?" Mal blinked. "What's that? Some kind of foreign food?"

"He's a composer," said Jake, shrugging to show this was new information for him, too.

Mal considered this. "Okay. I'm not upset anymore. I never would have come up with that. Elgar? Really? What planet was he from?"

They were in the reading room, their sheets and blankets folded and packed away for the day. Winston had showered and dressed, and the whole time Amanda's last-second steal of the breakfast puzzle was like a splinter in his brain. The letters had been right there on his notepad—if he'd simply read them out loud, without even knowing what he was saying, he would have won the prize. But no, he had to go scrambling letters that didn't need to be scrambled. He kept reliving the moment and getting annoyed all over again.

It must have shown on his face, because when Penrose came into the reading room, he patted Winston compassionately on the shoulder. Kimberly Schmidt, too, smiled and complimented him for solving the puzzle. "So you didn't recognize the answer," she said, shrugging. "I know who Elgar is, but I never would have come up with it, because I had no idea how to solve that thing."

The others filed into the reading room and found seats. The brats were acting surprisingly unbratty, pushing toy cars around the floor and making *vroom* noises. Their mother, Betty, took the opportunity to have a few minutes of quiet conversation with Larry Rossdale.

Winston glanced at Amanda and thought she looked pretty smug sitting there next to her mom. At least she looked happy to be here for a change. She was, after all, going to win some kind of prize. What would it be?

They were about to find out. Richard was the last to enter, and everyone quieted down as he said, "I hope you all had a good night's sleep and a fulfilling breakfast. And now I'd like to award the first prize of the day to Miss Amanda Deburgh."

Amanda's smile widened.

Richard said, "I've always felt a close affinity with Edward Elgar. In fact, I was born in 1934 the very same week that Elgar died. When I was a young man touring England, I played the Royal Albert

Hall. The manager presented me with a gift: a program from an El-gar concert, played exactly fifty years before my own debut there. And signed by the composer himself. It was a wonderful gift, and it became a cherished possession. And who better to pass it on to but another young pianist?"

"Wait a moment," said Gerard Deburgh. "That's the prize? That's what you're giving Amanda?"

"It is indeed."

Gerard sputtered out something that might have been a laugh. "Richard! You can't give something like that away. Even to my daugh-ter! A program signed by Elgar and owned by Richard Overton? That's too much!"

"Nonetheless," said Richard. He looked at Amanda and said, "I hope it provides you with some small measure of inspiration."

Amanda said thank you with a rather shocked expression on her face. Winston, to his surprise, was now relieved that he hadn't solved this morning's puzzle. What on earth would he have done with a valu-able, decades-old English concert program?

Norma stormed into the reading room wearing her severest frown yet. Richard saw her expression, and his pleasant smile faded away. Something was wrong.

She whispered into Richard's ear. "What?" he said.

Norma looked around at the assembled guests. Winston got the feeling she wished everyone would just go home. She said out loud, "The Elgar program is missing. It's not where it's supposed to be."

"It's in the entertainment room," Richard said. "I saw it there yesterday."

"I saw it there yesterday myself," Norma agreed. "But it is not there now."

"How very strange. Are you sure?"

Norma glared at her boss. Everyone understood her wordless response: *I am always sure.*

"Hmm," said Richard. "I'm sorry, Amanda, I guess there will be a slight delay in getting you your prize."

"It's too much, anyway!" said her father. "Richard, listen. You can't give something like that away. It's yours."

"Let me worry about that," said Richard.

Norma, unwilling to let the conversation drift too far, said, "But where is it? Who was in that room last night?" She looked around at the assembled guests, trying to find someone to accuse.

"You're not saying somebody stole it?" Larry said with some amazement.

Norma turned to him. "It didn't sprout wings and fly away, now, did it?"

She was being rude to the guests. Richard said, "Norma—"

"Perhaps someone moved it," Derek Bibb suggested. "Someone picked it up to look at it and put it down somewhere else."

"Where was it?" Larry asked. "Did someone sleep in that room last night?"

Norma said, "It's kept in the entertainment room downstairs, along with many other awards."

"Oh," said Chase Worthington.

He said it softly, but everyone heard it, and all eyes immediately went to him. "Oh, what?" Norma asked.

Chase pursed his lips and paled considerably. He turned to Zook, who had been sitting disinterestedly nearby. "Zook . . . do you have anything you want to tell us?"

Zook looked around, surprised and unhappy to find himself in the spotlight. "Who, me? I didn't take this thing. I've never even heard of Elman or Eljee or whatever his name is."

"You slept in that room last night . . . ," his father said.

"But I didn't take anything!" Zook shouted, his anger rising up as sudden as an earthquake. "You just don't trust me! That's the problem!" He got to his feet and stomped out of the room.

Chase stood up but did not follow his son. After a moment he sank back into his chair, rubbing his forehead with the heel of his hand. "I'm sorry," he said. "I'll see he returns it. He doesn't mean any harm. He's just . . ." Chase faded out, as if not sure himself what Zook was.

"Your son took it, then?" Norma asked.

"Probably. Probably." Chase looked very far from the confident lawyer he played on television. "Zook got picked up for shoplifting a couple of months ago. I don't know. He's angry all the time, and doesn't always think about what he's doing. . . ." He looked around. "I shouldn't be getting into this here."

"So it would be in his bag," Norma said.

Chase blinked. "Uh. Yes, that's probably a good guess."

She said, "Go get it, please."

People were starting to be embarrassed as Norma ordered this famous actor around like he was a schoolchild. Chase, for his part, accepted the order quietly. He stood up and walked out of the room.

Nobody knew what to say. Penrose asked in a gentle voice, "Was anything else missing, did you notice?"

"No," said Norma. "And I checked. That's where we keep most of his awards. The Grammys are still there, and so is his Laurel Tree."

"Laurel Tree?" Jake asked.

"It's an award for classical musicians. Very prestigious," Norma said. "That hasn't been taken, thank goodness."

"I'm sure there's a very good explanation for all of this," Richard said calmly. Norma made a barely audible harrumphing sound.

Chase reappeared in the doorway, looking unhappy. Zook stood behind him, a defiant expression on his long face.

Norma said, "Do you have it?"

Chase looked at his hands. "No, it wasn't there."

"I didn't take it," Zook said. "I saw it last night, but it wasn't there when I woke up this morning."

Norma's eyes narrowed. "You saw it last night? But you said before you've never heard of Edward Elgar."

"I didn't know what it *was*," Zook said with annoyance. "I was looking around at things before I went to bed. I noticed it but didn't really look at it. When I woke up this morning, it wasn't there. It's this big case with a glass front, right? About this big?" He held up his hands to describe something about the size of a dictionary.

"Why didn't you say so before?" Norma asked.

"I didn't know what you were talking about," Zook said. "And besides, everyone was so quick to *accuse* me . . ."

"It wasn't in his bag," Chase said quickly. "And I don't know where else it could be. Zook says he didn't take it, and . . . I believe him." Winston didn't think that was the most convincing declaration of trust ever. There was still plenty of doubt in Zook's father's eyes.

Larry spoke up. "Zook. You say it wasn't there when you woke up this morning?"

"That's right."

"Did you leave the room and come back and *then* it was missing?"

Zook thought about it. "No. It was gone right when I woke up."

Larry frowned and stroked his chin. His expression was serious, but his eyes gleamed happily. Winston remembered that Larry Rossdale, in addition to being a weatherman and busy spokesperson, had started writing mystery novels. "One more question," Larry said to Zook. "Was your door locked last night?"

"Yeah," answered Zook. "I locked it before I went to sleep."

Norma made a sound of disgust. "Why these questions?" she said. "This is an unnecessary distraction. The boy took it himself."

"I did not!" Zook said.

"That's enough," said Richard. He said it in a pleasant voice, but everyone could tell he meant it. "I'm not going to have the weekend sullied by this little incident." He stood up and looked around at his guests. "If you took the Elgar program, I'm going to ask that you return it. Just put it back on the shelf in the music room, and all will be forgiven." He nodded. "That's the last I hope to hear of this. And now, if you'll excuse me, Norma and I need to set up for the next puzzle. I'm going to ask you to stay out of the library. The rest of the house is yours." He stood up and left.

After a moment, Norma followed him, giving a final backward look at the assorted guests, a glare that said as clear as day, *I'm watching you people. Don't steal anything else.*

SO *STILL* WINSTON was unable to see Richard Overton's magnificent library. This was getting to be something of a joke. At least they would solve the next puzzle in there, so the waiting would soon be over. Unless somehow the next puzzle involved wearing blindfolds.

They sat around awhile, not sure what to do with themselves. At the now-cleared dining room table, Gerard Deburgh and his wife settled into a card game with Derek Bibb and Chase Worthington, while Kimberly Schmidt stood in the kitchen drinking coffee and reading the newspaper. Even stranger than hanging around all these famous people was how quickly Winston had gotten used to it.

Neither of the other kids their age—Amanda or Zook—were anywhere to be seen.

"We haven't been upstairs yet," said Winston.

"It's just bedrooms, I think," said Mal. "Nice staircase, though. Makes me want to ride down the banister. Think anyone would mind?"

"I think Norma would tear you into tiny pieces," Winston told him.

"Hey, we should go watch a movie," Jake said. He was as taken with the movie theater as Winston was with the library.

That was a pretty good idea, so they went downstairs. The door was closed, and Mal opened it slowly, expecting to interrupt somebody. The lights were on, but the theater was empty. The boys stepped in, smiling again at the magic of it all. There was a small stage, and the silvery-white movie screen stretched from one end to the other. It wasn't as large as the screen in a real theater, but it was still pretty big, and it was bordered on either side by rich red curtains.

Jake made his way up a narrow stairway and opened the door into the projectionist's booth. "Whoa, look at all this stuff!" he said.

Mal and Winston followed. Jake stood there with his eyes shining, admiring a sweet variety of video equipment. Richard Overton had a DVD player, an old videocassette player, and another device that none of the boys could identify. All of these were connected via a tangled nest of wires to some sort of gadget that beamed the picture out to the movie screen. Then there were two old-fashioned movie projectors, and stacked between them were a number of film reels. The whole back wall was taken up with movies in various formats. Winston immediately began poring through these, and after a few minutes, he started pulling out certain titles.

"I don't think we're going to have time to watch all of those," Mal said.

"That's not what I'm doing. Hang on . . ."

Winston's voice had that faraway sound that Mal and Jake both recognized. They glanced at each other and nodded. Winston had been taken captive by a puzzle idea.

The twelve movies listed here can be arranged into three groups of four so that each group of titles has something in common. (You don't need to have seen these movies to solve this puzzle.) Can you sort the movies correctly, and then place the three movies in the box into their proper groups?

ELLA ENCHANTED

ALL THAT JAZZ

THE BRIDGES OF MADISON COUNTY

MAMMA MIA!

AVATAR

MR. SMITH GOES TO WASHINGTON

THE TRUMAN SHOW

DOCTOR DOLITTLE

GATTACA

ROB ROY

MILDRED PIERCE

CASABLANCA

STAR WARS

ARTHUR

KING KONG

(Answer, page 244.)

"So how do we get this going?" Mal said, feeling around the various gadgets for some kind of switch.

"And what movie are we watching, anyway?" Winston asked.

"Nothing, if we can't get this stuff working," said Jake. "Aha, I think this is the light switch," he said, and suddenly they were plunged into darkness. The house lights and the overhead bulbs in the projection booth all went out at the same time. For all Winston knew, Jake had blacked out the entire mansion.

"Yes," came Mal's voice from the dark. "That was the light switch."

"Ugh, hang on, I lost it," Jake said. Winston heard him rustling around. Something metallic fell off a shelf and hit the floor.

"I got it!" Jake said. The lights came back on to reveal Amanda Deburgh standing in front of the movie screen. She was frozen in mid tiptoe—she'd been trying to get out the door without being seen. The boys stared at her. Where had she come from?

"What are you doing?" Mal called out. "Playing hide-and-seek?"

Amanda turned red. "No. Shut up. I was just looking around."

The boys left the projection room and walked back down the stairs. Winston looked around the theater, trying to figure it out. "Where were you?" he asked. "Behind the curtains?"

"So what if I was?" she asked.

"Well, what were you doing back there?" Jake asked.

"Nothing," she said. "None of your business!" She folded her arms as if daring them to question her further about this.

How weird was this girl? Weird enough not to bother with. Mal shrugged. "Suit yourself," he said.

Amanda looked confused that the boys had dropped the subject so suddenly, but she recovered and stormed to the door . . . which opened before she could touch it. Zook walked in and frowned when he saw everybody else in here. Winston once again said a silent word of thanks that Mal and Jake had come along this weekend. These other two were no fun at all.

"What are you doing?" Zook said. "I was going to watch a movie."

"That's what we're going to do," said Jake.

Zook sighed with annoyance. "Fine," he said, and turned around to leave. He couldn't possibly watch a movie *with* them, it seemed.

Amanda called out, "Did you really steal that thing? What did you do with it?"

Zook turned back again, sullen and angry. "I didn't steal anything. Not that I expect anybody around here to believe me."

Winston didn't believe him. Neither did Amanda, who said, "I won't tell anybody. I don't care."

"Yeah," said Zook. "It's only your prize that's missing."

"Sure," Jake said. "*Her* prize. The one she snatched away from Winston, you mean."

Amanda glared at him. "It's not my fault he's never heard of Elgar. Anyway, if I had known what the prize was going to be, I wouldn't have said anything. What do I want with some old music program?" She looked at Zook with a little smirk of a smile. "I just want to know how you did it, that's all. Where did you hide it?"

Zook hesitated, and Winston knew why. Amanda was pretty, and she was looking at Zook with shining eyes and a rare smile. But he shook his head. "I didn't take it, I didn't hide it, and I don't know where it is. Stop asking. Go watch your movie." He turned on his heel and left the theater.

Amanda was offended that she'd been lumped in with Winston and his friends. "I'm not watching a movie!" she shouted, and followed Zook out of the room, closing the door behind her.

There was a small silence as the boys recovered from all that. Jake laughed, and Mal said, "They're a fun couple. We should hang out with them more often."

"I wonder what she was doing." Winston hoisted himself up on the small stage, and peeked behind the red curtains. There was nothing to see but darkness and dust. He took a couple of steps farther and felt the cool stone wall. "What a weird place to hide," he said.

"Maybe she wasn't hiding," Jake said. "Maybe she was looking for the thing Zook stole."

"That makes sense," Mal said. "Zook's room is right down the hall. He doesn't want to put the program in his bag, because what if someone looks in there? So he hides it somewhere else." He looked around. "This is a pretty good place for that."

"Except it's not here," Jake said, looking behind the curtains as well.

"Sure," said Mal. "But Amanda thought it was. That's why she was back there looking for it."

It was as good an explanation as any. Winston hopped off the stage. "I don't get why Zook would steal an old music program in the first place."

Jake said, "Did you see Amanda's father? He acted like Richard Overton wanted to give his daughter a million-dollar check. Maybe that thing is worth a lot of money."

"I guess," Winston said. "It just seems strange that Zook would know that." From what he could see, Zook's taste in music ran more toward loud electric guitars. "Come on," he said. "I want to see something." He left the theater.

The door to the entertainment room was closed, and Winston opened it slowly, worried that Zook might be in there. He wasn't— but Larry Rossdale was. Larry whirled around, surprised, as if Winston had caught him at something. It was an odd moment, seeing the morning news weatherman standing in front of the television instead of inside it.

Larry recovered from his surprise and laughed his trademark

Happy Weatherman laugh. "Hi, boys!" Larry said. "Would you like to put on some music or watch TV? Go ahead, I was just leaving."

All three boys sensed that Larry was up to something, but only Jake put his finger on what that was. "Are you looking for the thing Zook stole?" he asked.

Larry laughed again, and turned slightly pink. "Sort of, sort of," he said. "I just wanted to look around a little. This has the makings of a wonderful mystery, don't you think?"

Mal said, "You don't think Zook took it?"

"Oh . . . well." Larry looked around, leaned in, and said in a low voice, "He probably did." He then regained his usual cheerful excitement. "But if you assume for a moment that he *didn't*, then what you've got is a lovely locked-room mystery."

"A what?" Winston said.

"Think about it," Larry said. "We have a room, right?" He swung his arm to demonstrate that they were, indeed, in a room. "The door is locked, and inside is a sleeping person."

"Yeah . . ."

"A sleeping person in a locked room! So if Zook didn't take the program, the question is not only 'whodunit' but also how could the thief steal the program at all? He had to get into a locked room without waking up the person inside, steal the thing, and get out again. A locked-room mystery!"

They thought about that. Mal said, "I think all you're doing is proving that Zook stole it himself."

"Yeah," Winston agreed. "This isn't a whodunit. It's a where-did-it-go?"

They looked around. The couch where Zook slept was still covered with a rumpled sheet and unfolded blanket. His bag was next to the sofa, and various articles of clothing were strewn around it.

Winston examined the wide variety of memorabilia that Richard kept here. There were photographs of the pianist standing next to presidents and celebrities, and all kinds of awards, including three Grammys. Near the end of the long shelf was a conspicuous gap.

"Well, that's where the program was," said Mal.

"Sure," said Larry. "Good eye!"

"So where did he hide it?" Jake asked.

There was a closet at the far end of the long shelf. Winston opened it and looked inside. It was pretty deep, with a long horizontal bar for hanging stuff and, behind that, shelves that held pillows and blankets. Winston moved things around a little and found nothing. "It's not in here," he said.

Norma opened the door and poked her head in. Her eyes flicked around the room, instinctively checking to see if another crime was in progress. Satisfied that nothing else was being stolen, she said, "The second puzzle will begin momentarily. Please gather in the library."

Larry smiled broadly. "Okay, Norma! Thanks!"

They started out of the entertainment room and down the hall. As they walked, Jake got curious, and said to Larry, "So if it wasn't Zook, how could someone else have gotten in there? How do you steal something from a locked room?"

Larry shook his head. "I don't know. I'm trying to think like a mystery writer—"

"Which you *are*," Mal reminded him.

"Well, I'm just starting out. And right now I don't have any idea how a person could steal something from that room if it was locked."

"Maybe somebody had the key," Winston said.

Larry shook his head. "There's no keyhole. There's a little hole in the doorknob so you can pick the lock in an emergency. I guess somebody could have done that, but wouldn't they have woken up Zook in the process?"

"Through the window, maybe?" Jake said.

Mal said, "Duh, Jake. We're in the basement."

"Oh. Right."

"Yes," Larry said. "No windows down here." He shrugged extravagantly. "Like you said, Chase's son almost certainly did this himself. It'd sure be fun, though, if somebody else did it, in some creative, diabolical way."

They chatted until they reached the library. Stepping in at last, Winston stopped in his tracks, openmouthed. It was enormous—big enough that Winston's brain almost refused to accept it. Coming from the bland, carpeted hallway into this gaping underground cavern filled with bookshelves was like discovering a three-ring circus in your living room. It was impossible that all this could be in someone's house, even if it was a large house.

Penrose greeted the boys. "Enjoying yourselves?" He saw the expression on Winston's face and smiled as if he'd once had a similar reaction.

Larry laughed. "You can always tell when someone is visiting this place for the first time. It's something, isn't it?"

Winston nodded mutely. Three of the four walls were lined with bookcases. More bookshelves were strategically placed here and there, among long tables and an assortment of chairs. And then on top of all that, two staircases—one on either side—led up to a second floor. The second floor of the library consisted of a huge indoor balcony, wrapping around the four walls, with only a narrow foot or two of floor space between the bookshelves and the railing.

Richard was standing midway up one of the staircases, so he

could see everybody come in. "Hello again!" he called. "Welcome to the second puzzle of the weekend! You'll notice how I'm doing all of you a favor this time and actually telling you that the puzzle has started."

"We appreciate that," said Chase Worthington, and there was some mild laughter.

"The puzzle is here in my library," said Richard. "Finding it, however, is up to you." At once, heads turned in all directions, as if the puzzle were fluttering around them like butterflies.

Richard continued. "There are eight different puzzle pieces, hidden all around. When you find a piece, please leave it so that others may find it, too. I've left some pads of paper and pencils for you, if you need to take notes. The answer to this puzzle is a four-letter word. The first person to say that word to me shall be the winner. Are you ready?"

They were ready.

"Then, go!"

THE GUESTS SCATTERED excitedly, heading off in all directions. Betty McGinley had her brats with her, and the two kids were, for the moment, well-behaved. They understood that this was a game of hide-and-seek, and they were eager to play. It was more surprising to see Zook trailing after his father. He wasn't doing cartwheels of enthusiasm, but he wasn't complaining, either.

Jake picked up some paper and a pencil. "I guess we're all working by ourselves?" he said.

"I guess we are," Winston agreed.

"All right, then." Jake grinned. "I'll race ya." He headed for one of the staircases.

"If this was a running race," Mal said, "I would just give up now. But I always was good at Easter egg hunts." He jogged away and rounded a corner behind one of the bookshelves.

Winston didn't know where to begin, so he set off at random, walking between the bookshelves, examining the walls. He found himself next to Penrose, who was staring with great concentration at a painting.

"What are we looking for?" Winston asked.

"I can't really tell yet, I'm afraid." Penrose's glasses were at the tip of his nose as he studied the painting, which was hung in the narrow space between sets of bookshelves. "I can't remember if this painting has always been here or not," Penrose said. It was a perfectly nice piece of artwork, but Winston didn't think there was anything puzzly about it. He kept going.

Winston reached the back of the library, where he found another framed work in a gap between the shelves. This time it was a strange ink drawing. Unlike the painting, this one looked *very* puzzly:

A fishing rod, and then a musical note, and then the letter O. Or was that a zero? No, Winston thought it was an O. What could it mean? Maybe there was no way to know—not until he found some of the other puzzle pieces. But Winston couldn't tear himself away from this piece yet. It was a mystery that demanded solving.

"I always enjoy these weekends," said a voice behind him. Winston turned, and Kimberly Schmidt was there. "But one thing I have learned over the years is I am very bad at puzzles." Her eyebrows were furrowed in the direction of the puzzle on the wall, a frown on her pretty face. "What do you think this is?"

"I don't know yet," Winston admitted. "A picture puzzle of some kind."

"A message, maybe," Kimberly said. She waved a hand like a queen about to make a pronouncement: "Fishing for music!" she exclaimed. "Plus the letter O."

Winston smiled. "That's probably not it."

"And what's with the blanks?" She moved closer to get a better look. "Does that mean the answer is five letters? But Richard said the answer is *four* letters."

Winston thought about that and said, "Well, the answer to this *part* of the puzzle could be five letters. So maybe each of the eight puzzle pieces will lead to a different word. Then we'll have to combine those words in some way."

Kimberly shook her head. "I think I'm going to stick to the cello."

They continued to stare at the drawing, Winston enjoying the beautiful musician's company.

"What note is that, anyway?" he asked.

"It's an E," said Kimberly. "Is that important?"

"Might be," Winston said, staring, and less than a second later, the answer buzzed into his brain. "In fact, yes!" he said, and quickly wrote something down on his pad.

"You've got it?"

"I do." Winston beamed.

She crinkled her eyes at him. "You're not going to tell me the answer, are you?"

"Well," said Winston. "If you really want to know . . ."

Kimberly laughed. "I'll try to work it out," she said. "If I need help, I know where to find you."

They smiled a good-bye at each other, and Winston went off to find more puzzle pieces. When he looked back, Kimberly was still there, hands on hips, staring at the picture of the fishing rod.

It took Winston a solid twenty minutes to find the rest of the pieces—some of them had been hung in very tricky places. In one case, Richard had placed the frame face-out on the bottommost shelf of a bookcase. Winston must have walked by that one half a dozen times. Another clue was hidden underneath one of the staircases leading to the second floor. He only found that one thanks to the brats yelling, "Here it is, Mommy!" Winston saw Richard wince as his clever hiding spot was revealed for one and all.

Winston found all eight clues, but was missing a few of the answers. One of the pictures in the clues was very peculiar—it was simply a list of all of their names. What could that mean? He took a seat at one of the tables and studied the notes he had taken.

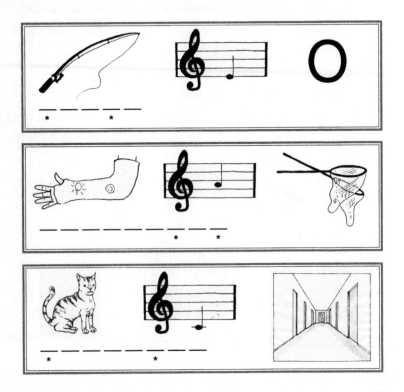

_ _ _ _ _
   *   *

Arthur   Mal
Gerard   Jake
Candice   Larry
Amanda Derek
Chase   Kimberly
Zook   Betty
Winston

_ _ _ _ _
  * *

_ _ _ _ _ _ _
   *   *

note after sol

_ _ _ _ _ _
     *   *

(Continue reading to see the answer to this puzzle.)

Winston took an aggravated breath as he studied the papers in front of him. He was most of the way to the answer, but couldn't drag himself across the finish line. What was he missing?

It was clear that each of these pieces was a rebus—that first puzzle he'd found was a fishing rod, an E note, and then the letter O. ROD + E + O = RODEO, a five-letter word to match the five blanks. The first and fourth letters of the answer were marked with stars, so Winston assumed he only needed the R and E.

After some staring, he'd figured out all of the other rebuses, and now he had a little chart in front of him:

RODEO	RE
CASTANETS	ES
CATCHALL	CA
BONUS	OU
ATONED	TO
CANDIDATE	ND
BEEPING	IN
FLARING	NG

The last rebus he solved was the one that showed all of their names—Winston had thought that one would drive him crazy. The first part was a B note, then came the word ON, and then . . . NAMES? BONNAMES? That wasn't a word. He had stared at it, his mouth opening and closing around a thousand wrong answers, and then at last the lightbulb came on: Who were those people? Why, they were US! So the answer had to be B-ON-US. Bonus!

Now he had two letters from each answer. But what was he supposed to do with them? Could he rearrange them so that they spelled something? Maybe. But after writing and erasing the letters a million times, Winston had to admit he couldn't figure it out. He looked around the room and saw a couple of other guests sitting or standing with their own notepads. They too were stuck on this last step. Gerard Deburgh muttered to himself while he scribbled on his pad. He looked like somebody would take away all his restaurants if he didn't solve this puzzle. Candice Deburgh and Amanda were up on the second floor—they were working together, without Gerard, who perhaps was too intense a teammate.

Winston got up and started to pace. The answer wasn't coming to him here. Maybe it would come to him somewhere else.

He walked and thought, and occasionally stopped to jot down an idea on his notepad. The answer continued its little practical joke, staying inches out of reach. He stared at the pairs of letters and mentally begged them to form something sensible. The letters refused.

Mal had given up on the puzzle—he had found an interesting book and was standing there reading it. He looked up as Winston walked over, and made a face to show his frustration.

"How far did you get?" Winston asked.

"I found all the clues," said Mal, "and I know they're all rebuses. I couldn't solve a couple of them." He glanced at the paper in Winston's hand. "BONUS! So that's what that one is. Geez!"

Winston held his notes up to his chest. "Yell the answers a little louder, why don't you?"

"Sorry," Mal said. "That one was making me nuts."

Jake came up to them looking like he wanted to kick something.

"There are really eight clues in here somewhere? Did you guys find them all?"

"I did," Mal said. "For all the good it did me."

"I got them all, and I solved them," said Winston, "but I don't know what to do next. Do you want to see?"

Both his friends did, so Winston showed them his list:

RODEO	RE
CASTANETS	ES
CATCHALL	CA
BONUS	OU
ATONED	TO
CANDIDATE	ND
BEEPING	IN
FLARING	NG

Mal's habit when presented with a bunch of letters that didn't spell anything was to pronounce them out loud anyway. "Reescaoutondinng!" he intoned, like a wizard reading from a spellbook.

"I think that's more than four letters," Jake said.

"You have to rearrange all this to get the real answer," said Winston, "but I'm not getting anywhere with it."

The three of them frowned at the words for a bit.

"Are you sure?" said Mal after a while. "Maybe there's something else you have to do. Because I'm not seeing anything here."

"I see the word TOES," said Jake. "That's about it."

Winston shook his head. "I don't know. Maybe Mal's right. Maybe there's another step to this." He walked over to the nearest puzzle piece and stared at it again.

"I liked this one," said Jake. "Probably because I got it real fast. Castanets! Easy."

"This is the first one I found," said Mal, "so then I thought all the answers were going to be musical instruments. Boy, that screwed me up for a while."

Winston said thoughtfully, "They're not all instruments . . . but each of the puzzles does have a musical note." He stared at the puzzle and then back at what he had written down.

Lightning struck his brain. The big *aha!* moment was never a slow, creeping thing—it always leapt out of nowhere like a surprise party. As usual, there was a moment where he lost his breath entirely. He'd been waiting for a breakthrough. Here it was.

He shouted something unintelligible but happy, and ran for a table so he could sit down, leaving Mal and Jake to stare at each other with amusement.

"I think he's got it," said Mal.

"Not yet, not yet," said Winston. "But look at this." The boys went over and watched as he added a new column to his notes:

E	RODEO	RE
A	CASTANETS	ES
MIDDLE C	CATCHALL	CA
B	BONUS	OU
D	ATONED	TO
HIGH C	CANDIDATE	ND
G	BEEPING	IN
F	FLARING	NG

"The musical notes are all different. Is that important?" Jake said.

"Yep!" Winston said happily. "That's the final clue you need."

(Continue reading to see the answer to this puzzle.)

Winston knew how to get the answer, but he still had to do the work. He leaned forward, writing quickly, rearranging the letters as instructed by the musical notes—starting with middle C and working his way up through the eight notes of the musical scale. When put in that order, a message appeared, clear as day: CAT OR ENGINE SOUND.

Aha! Winston thought, and stood up to find Richard.

But before he could take a single step, Richard said, "My friends, we have a winner!" Winston looked around with dumb surprise: *How did Richard know I solved the puzzle? I haven't even gotten to him yet.* But, no. It was the theater director, Derek Bibb, who had reached Richard first with the answer. Richard was patting Derek on the shoulder in congratulations, and there was a polite round of applause. Derek bowed humbly, looking pleased.

Jake saw the stunned expression on Winston's face. "Sorry, Win," he said.

Richard was still talking. He explained to the others how to find the answer phrase, and there was laughter and some smacking of foreheads from the other guests. "And what is a four-letter word meaning 'cat or engine sound'?" Richard asked.

"Purr!" shouted most everybody.

"That's absolutely right," said Richard. "And, Derek, because you were the first to arrive at the answer, you get the prize. Norma?"

Norma came forward holding a framed painting, covered with a black cloth. Richard eased it away from her and placed it on the table, angling it so that everybody could see.

He said, "You all know how I admire the paintings of Sutton Hammill, who enjoys puzzles almost as much as I do. I have a few of his original works, and Derek, I am giving this one to you."

Derek looked shocked. "Richard . . . thank you. Are you sure?"

"Of course I am sure," Richard said, and he flipped over the black cloth, revealing the painting. Winston leaned in and squinted, because he couldn't tell what he was looking at.

Neither could anybody else, apparently. "What . . . what is it?" asked Chase.

Richard smiled. "It's a cat."

"It is?"

"But the pieces are out of order. It's up to you to put it back together again with your eyes."

(Answer, page 245.)

Winston, grumpier than ever, was sitting upstairs in the reading room. This time he made no attempt to hide his irritation: He sat with his arms crossed, frowning at the floor. Fine, the breakfast puzzle had been stolen away at the last second. Things like that happen. But now he'd come an inch short on a *second* puzzle, and that one would have earned him a far cooler prize.

If his sister were acting like this, he'd call her a sore loser. He knew that, but he couldn't help it. Two puzzles in a row!

Mal came over, looked in the direction Winston was staring, and saw nothing. He asked, "Is there an invisible puzzle over there that you're trying to solve?"

Winston grunted annoyance, and Mal decided maybe this wasn't a good time for jokes. He sat down and gazed out the window at the wide, lush lawn. Jake came in from the direction of the kitchen, eating an apple. "This place has everything," he said, "except potato chips."

"I think I heard Norma say they were ordering in lunch," Mal said.

"Can't we just eat last night's dinner again?"

"I know, really!" said Mal. "When I get rich, the first thing I'm gonna do is hire a cook."

Jake noticed Winston and said, "He okay?"

Mal said, "He's tired of puzzles. He's vowing to never solve them again."

Winston said mopily, "Maybe I should."

His friends looked at him with blank surprise. Mal leaned in and said, "Winston? Is that you?"

"He's kidding," Jake said. He considered Winston for a moment and added, "Right?"

Winston shrugged. He didn't think he could walk away from

puzzles—not really—but right at the moment, it didn't seem like a terrible idea.

Mal looked around the room like someone in a fog. "I must be dreaming. This can't be a real conversation. When I said you were giving up puzzles, that was a *joke.*"

"Is this because of the puzzles we've had so far?" Jake asked. He wasn't goofing around like Mal, but he too looked like he thought Winston might have been replaced by an alien. "You got burned twice," he said, "but you have to get right back in there. That's what my coaches would tell me."

"It's not because of the puzzles today," Winston said, though it probably was, at least in part. He told them about the trouble he'd gotten into at school, and about the puzzle event from a few weeks back, the one where he'd sat in his room all day, and how when it was over he'd felt like a trick-or-treater who has eaten too much Halloween candy. And then, on top of that, he'd missed out on seeing Adventureland with them.

Jake gritted his teeth, embarrassed. "I'm sorry," he said. "I would have invited you, but I knew you were busy. I actually thought it would be sort of mean to tell you what you were missing."

That made an aggravating sort of sense. Winston sighed.

"But still!" Mal said. "You can't give up puzzles. That'd be like me giving up—"

"Having a big mouth," Jake concluded for him.

"Yeah!" Mal agreed. He wasn't insulted. He knew the truth when he heard it.

Winston laughed before he even realized it, and then he laughed again. He felt a little better. He decided he didn't want to mope around all weekend. That was Zook's job.

He had to admit, though . . . something was still nibbling at him.

Something about puzzles. He'd been solving them forever, but it was hard not to notice that lately they were tripping him up, getting in his way. It was like having an untrained dog inside his head, one that was friendly but constantly demanding attention. He wondered—only briefly—what it might be like if he *did* give up puzzles. Could he even do it? He didn't know, but it spooked him a little that he'd had the thought.

One of the brats came running in, shouting, "Lollipop! Lollipop!" Their mother, Betty, followed at a run, saying, "I *told* you, not until after lunch." But the child had already reached his mother's purse, which had been placed on a chair. He grabbed it and sent it tumbling, spilling its contents all over.

"Ugh! Ryan!" Betty shouted, and knelt down to gather her belongings. Winston wondered where Ryan's brother was. Either of these kids off by himself was bad news. And sure enough, at just that moment, he heard Norma yell from the kitchen, "Ian! Please don't touch that! No!" These kids were part human, part wrecking ball.

Betty picked up her wallet, which had unfolded itself as it hit the floor. She peered into it as she gathered it up, and did a double take. She looked around, flustered and upset. "Did you get into Mommy's wallet?" Betty asked Ryan, who had found a lollipop and was fighting with the wrapper. She looked around again, her agitation growing. Finally her eyes set on Winston and his friends, sitting on the other side of the room.

"Did you see anyone go into my bag?" she asked.

The boys all shook their heads. "No," said Jake. "I didn't even notice it sitting there."

"Well, somebody did," Betty said, her puzzlement giving way to anger. "I had over three hundred dollars cash in here. And now it's gone."

IT WAS HARD keeping the mood light as they sat around eating the sandwiches Norma had ordered in, but Richard was determined to try. He had plenty of assistance from Larry Rossdale, who could be counted on to bellow merry laughter at just about anything. Winston could tell, though, that people were disturbed. It was getting harder to ignore the fact that one of the party guests was a thief.

At first, all attention once again turned to Zook. But under his father's questioning, Zook replied hotly, "When did I do it? I was with you the whole time, playing treasure hunt in the library. Besides, I'd have to be pretty stupid to steal money when everybody already thinks I stole this other thing. Which I *didn't*."

Everybody grudgingly agreed that Zook had been in the library during the entire puzzle. Of course, he could have stolen the money before then, but when Gerard Deburgh brought that up, Kimberly Schmidt observed that from the end of breakfast onward, there were always a few people in the reading room—somebody would have seen him do it. Nobody knew what to say to that, and then lunch arrived, so the whole thing was dropped, at least for the moment.

Zook was no longer glowering with anger. Sitting next to his father in a pair of wingback chairs, a paper plate on his lap, he only looked tired of being accused of every bad thing that happened around here. Winston halfway felt bad for him and halfway thought he really was the thief. Chase Worthington had even gone so far as to offer Betty McGinley the money out of his own pocket, which made Zook exhale an irritated breath. Betty turned down the money.

Winston and his friends were back at the dining room table. Derek Bibb was sitting there, and Mal—now that he had fully recovered from Derek's presence—wanted to ask the famous director questions about theater and acting. For the first time, it occurred to Winston that Mal wasn't joking about wanting to be an actor someday.

Winston tuned out of their conversation pretty quickly. He chatted in a low voice with Jake about Zook: Why would he have stolen the money, if indeed he had? His father was the star of a successful television show—surely Zook could buy anything he wanted. And yet his father mentioned how Zook had been caught shoplifting not too long before. Whatever Zook was up to, it had nothing to do with money and everything to do with being an all-around ticked-off jerk.

And, really, if Zook wasn't the thief, who was? *Everybody* around here was richer than Winston could imagine. Did Gerard Deburgh, or even Amanda, need three hundred dollars snatched from a random pocketbook? Heck, no. Deburgh was a multibazillionaire businessman. Who did that leave as a suspect? The world-famous cello player? The theater director with a play on Broadway? The weatherman who made barrels of money pitching products on television? It was crazy to think any of them had done it.

Well, Penrose wasn't rich. But he probably wasn't poor, either—not if he traveled to other countries as frequently as he did. "Even if Penrose was dead broke," said Jake, "no way is he the thief." Winston agreed. *Penrose?* Rifling through somebody's wallet and stealing the cash? That was ridiculous.

Winston was worried that maybe someone would turn the spotlight on *him*, or Mal or Jake. Of all the guests in attendance, the three of them were the most likely to think three hundred dollars was a lot of money. And for a while they *had* been sitting in the same room as the purse. But, to Winston's relief, nobody thought to grill them about the theft. Most of the guests, taking a cue from Richard, only wanted to forget anything had happened.

Winston glanced over to see that Derek was back in lecture mode again, this time for an audience of one. Mal looked a little glassy-eyed. He glanced over to his friends, and his expression asked the question, *What have I gotten myself into?*

The deck of cards was still out. While they waited for Derek to wind down, Winston found himself cutting and shuffling the deck, and then idly flipping through the cards, removing some, putting others back into the deck, arranging things in some way. Jake watched him with increasing amusement. "Yeah," he said. "You can give up puzzles. I believe that."

Winston looked at what he was doing, and blinked in surprise. Jake was right. Winston had been absently turning the cards into a puzzle. His brain was on puzzling autopilot.

Without moving these cards, can you divide them into two equal groups so that both groups have the same number of hearts and the same number of diamonds?

(Answer, page 245.)

The sun had come out, taking the edge off the morning's chill. And that was good, because the third puzzle was to be held outside, in Richard Overton's extensive garden.

"If we have to identify flowers," Gerard Deburgh said, "I'll just stay here and read the paper."

Richard assured him it was nothing of the kind, so Gerard and the rest of them put on their jackets, grabbed pencils and paper, and gathered outside the front door. Norma stayed behind. She had taken Richard aside and suggested—in a whisper that was nonetheless loud enough for everyone to hear—that the rest of the puzzles be canceled. Why continue with a party when one of the guests was a thief? Richard refused to listen.

He led them around to the garden that Winston had spied from a distance last evening. Like Gerard, Winston didn't know many different kinds of flowers. But there seemed to be hundreds in Richard's garden. The entrance was guarded on either side by tall, odd-looking flowers in giant ceramic pots—Winston didn't realize it was possible for a flower to look proud of itself, but these purple flowers looked ready to sing their own praises.

"Oh, these orchids are beautiful!" Kimberly exclaimed, and Richard thanked her, obviously pleased.

Next to each pot was a park bench, the wooden slats set into an ornate metal framework. In the garden itself, paths cut this way and that through the brightly colored flowers and the lush greenery, and Richard smiled as his guests oohed and aahed at the sight of it all. "I had Freddie working double time over the last few weeks, getting the garden ready for today," Richard said. "He's done a wonderful job, don't you think?" No one could disagree.

Richard continued, "Here's another puzzle where you'll have to wander around a little. You'll need to explore my garden in search of . . . well, you'll soon find out. Then it will be up to you to figure out what to do. Make sure you follow every path. Your answer will be a six-letter word. But keep these numbers in mind as well: nine, eight, six. That's a little hint for all of you."

"Not much of a hint," Mal said to Winston. "Nine eight six? What does it mean?"

"I guess we'll see," said Winston.

"Wanna stick together?" Jake asked.

"Sure thing," Mal said. So the boys headed down one of the paths.

"Learn a lot from Derek Bibb?" Winston asked.

"Oh, man," Mal said, looking around to see if Derek was nearby. "The guy's really smart, no doubt about that. But talking to him is like sinking in quicksand."

"Next time we'll throw you a rope," Jake said.

It didn't take long to discover what Richard was up to. Down the first path was a little clearing. In the center was a wooden post with a sign showing a single letter: O.

"Aha!" said Mal. "I know what to do for a change! It's a maze, and we have to spell out a message as we go along!"

"That sounds pretty good," Winston said. "But which way are we supposed to go now?" There were four paths out of this clearing—the one they had come from, and three others, heading off at various angles into the garden.

"Hey, I'm just the idea man," said Mal. "I'll let you take it from here."

So they headed down a path at random, looking at different kinds of plants, until they reached another clearing and another signpost. This one displayed the letter N. Jake wrote it diligently on his notepad. Winston wasn't taking notes yet. He needed to see more before he felt confident they were on the right track.

There were three paths away from this point, and again they chose one for no particular reason. This time they found themselves in a slightly larger clearing, though still with a single signpost at the center. Jake wrote down the letter E in his notepad. The E, Winston noticed, was larger than the other letters and painted red instead of black. It also had a red circle painted around it.

"Wow. Now what?" Jake said, looking around. There were no fewer than seven paths leading away.

"We're supposed to take every path, isn't that what he said?" Winston asked.

"Yes," Mal agreed. "Quick. Everybody clone yourself."

Candice Deburgh and Amanda came up from one of the other paths. Gerard wasn't with them. Winston remembered that Gerard had worked by himself during the library puzzle, too. Did he not want to solve with his wife and daughter, or did they not want to work with him?

Amanda looked around at the many paths and made an annoyed sound. "How are we supposed to know where to go next?"

"I think that's part of the puzzle," Jake said.

"Well, it's hard to believe I'm going to solve this," said Amanda's mother, "but this garden is certainly lovely. Oh, look!" She stepped happily over to examine a bunch of flowers that resembled lavender-colored popcorn, while Amanda stood there looking impatient.

"Come on, let's keep going," Jake said, and chose the next path for them. It led to a sign marked with a V, and there was only one way to continue out of that clearing, so they kept going straight until they reached another sign, this one with a capital letter I. Derek Bibb and Mr. Penrose were here, examining the sign closely, like it contained a whole secret language instead of a single letter. Mal, formerly Derek's biggest fan, looked wary, but the lecture was officially over. The theater director was now interested only in the puzzle.

Penrose was shaking his head. "I don't see that we're spelling anything useful."

"Could it be something else?" asked Derek. "Perhaps we need to travel to each letter in order."

Penrose frowned. "How would that work?" he asked. "We have S and I in consecutive clearings. Last I checked, they aren't next to each other in the alphabet."

"You found an S?" Jake asked.

"Yes, up that way," Derek said, pointing. "Where did you boys come from?"

"From thataway," Mal said, gesturing behind them. "There's a V back there."

There was only one other way out of this clearing. Shrugging, Derek said, "Shall we?" So the five of them marched down the path. Winston noticed for the first time that all of these pathways were perfectly straight—not a curve to be seen anywhere. Was that important? Maybe, although Winston couldn't see how.

They arrived at a clearing. The sign here showed the letter L.

"Evil!" shouted Mal, so suddenly that everybody jumped.

"He's right," Jake said. "We just spelled the word EVIL. Except before that we had an O and an N."

"On evil!" Mal said. "I don't know what it means, but it's gotta be something."

Derek said, "But we took a different set of paths and have a completely different set of letters. Who's to say who is right?"

"What letters do you have?" Winston asked.

"T, S, I, and now L," Penrose said, referring to his notepad.

"At least our letters spell something," said Mal.

There was only one other path out of here, so they kept going. The boys walked slower than usual, because Penrose's jogging days were behind him. As they walked, Jake said to Winston, "So tell me you're not enjoying this."

Winston knew what Jake was getting at. He shrugged. "I am. Of course I am."

"So you still want to give up puzzles?"

Penrose looked at them, his eyes wide behind his glasses. "What is this?" he asked.

Mal said, "Winston wants to give up puzzles and become a football player or something."

"I never said anything about being a football player!" Winston said a little too loudly. "I don't want to give up puzzles, either," he said, and then surprised himself by adding, "I don't think." He didn't really want to talk about this and wished Jake and Mal would stop bringing it up. His own thoughts were still too confused. His friends sensed this, and backed off. So did Penrose, though the curious and concerned expression did not leave his face.

They arrived at the next clearing, and Jake said, "Whoops."

"Whoops what?"

"Whoops we've been here before." He pointed at the O on the signpost. "This is the first letter we saw."

They all thought about that. Derek said, "It's not the first letter *we* saw. Our first letter was a T. I think it's over this way." He pointed down the path that led back to the garden's entrance. Beyond that, the path continued into another clearing.

"So that way is the T," Mal said. "This way is the N that we already saw. We just came from the L in this direction. That leaves one more path out of here." He pointed, and the group continued to walk together. This path didn't go on for very long before they reached another clearing. The sign here said P.

Looking at it, Derek said, "I think it would be splendid if I had some idea what I was doing."

"We have to spell something," said Penrose. "Don't you think?"

"Sure," said Jake, "but there are a million ways to take these different paths. We could be walking in here forever."

"Hey, we spelled the word EVIL," Mal reminded him.

Jake shook his head. "I think we just got lucky. I don't think that means anything."

"Wait," Winston said. "Don't forget about the hint he gave us. What were those numbers again?"

"Nine, eight, six," Mal said.

Winston nodded. "So the answer is going to be three words. A nine-letter word . . ."

Jake got it. "Then an eight-letter word, then a six-letter word."

"Right."

"How does that help us figure out what the answer *is*?" Mal asked.

"Here's what I think," Winston said, and he flipped to a new page in his notepad. He spent some time scribbling letters and circles. "I've seen this kind of puzzle before," he said. "Just not life-size, so it took me a while to recognize it. Here's how a puzzle like this would work on paper."

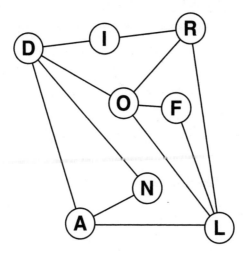

"Starting from one of these circles," Winston said, "you can trace out the name of a large city and the state it's in. Both the city and the state are seven letters long. You'll use every pathway at least once."

(Answer, page 246.)

"So it's not enough to walk around the garden looking at letters," Derek Bibb said. "We have to make a map."

"Yes, I think so," said Winston. "The letters and the paths."

"Yikes," said Mal, looking around.

They all contemplated the difficulty of the task ahead, and then Penrose clapped sharply. "Well. The best way to start is to start, wouldn't you say?"

"Maybe we should split up," Jake said.

"Exactly what I was going to suggest," said Derek. "We can head off in various directions, then meet back here. Or at the entrance. Yes, let's meet back at the garden entrance in fifteen minutes and compare notes."

There were five of them and only three paths out of the clearing, so they broke into smaller groups: Derek went off on his own, Jake and Mal went another way, and Penrose and Winston took the third path.

"So, what were your friends talking about?" Penrose asked as they walked. "Something about not wanting to solve puzzles anymore? That's hard to believe."

Winston didn't want to get into it all over again—the trouble with his teachers, missing out on Adventureland—so he said, "I don't know. I guess I wondered what it would be like to do something different."

"Like what?"

"Well . . . ," Winston said. That was the problem, wasn't it? He had no idea.

Penrose saw the blankness on Winston's face and smiled. "I think you might wait to give up your passion until something comes along to replace it. My opinion is, you can't wake up one morning and decide to become a stamp collector. Or a gardener!" he said, sweeping an arm at the greenery around them. "You have to *want* to do these things, on a deeper level." He made an old, wrinkled fist and tapped himself several times below his rib cage.

"I guess that's true," Winston said. Right at the moment, he wasn't sure what he wanted.

They walked through a few clearings, and Winston carefully noted down the letters and the paths. Penrose then said he was getting tired, and he would meet Winston back at the garden entrance. "I'm glad we are working on something together, Winston," he said. "I was hoping we would before the weekend was over." He shuffled off.

Winston could now go a lot faster, and did. He got interested looks—*what is he up to?*—from Gerard and Kimberly as he raced past them, trying to run and write in his notebook at the same time. Whether or not he'd be solving puzzles tomorrow, he was certainly enjoying this one right now. He didn't get to cover every path, but he did pretty well, and he arrived back at the garden entrance with a good idea of how the map would work.

The brats were there, being reprimanded—not by their mother but by Derek. His lecture this time was not about theater, but about manners. The boys, downcast, were sitting on one of the benches, their hands and faces covered in dirt. They'd been having a dirt fight—throwing clumps of soil from the two large flowerpots at each other. One of the two orchids was leaning to the side, fainting in slow motion. Penrose sat on the other bench, shaking his head in disbelief.

Betty came running out of the garden. "Oh, no!" she said. "I stepped away for less than five minutes . . . ! I'm so sorry." She looked at the damaged orchid and seemed almost about to cry. Then she rounded on her boys. "Didn't I ask you to behave? Can't I leave you for a minute? You get back to the house right now. We are getting you washed up, and when we get back home, the two of you are going to be *punished*—" She continued in this vein for some time, until both boys started crying. It was a relief when the three of them left for the house. Richard had insisted she come, sure, but how much game playing did Betty McGinley think she was going to do this weekend, with those two travel-size demons alongside her?

"What a shame," Derek said of the fallen flower. He tried straightening it up, to no avail. Richard came out of the garden, looking concerned, and Winston saw his face fall when he saw the damaged orchid. "Betty's kids," Derek said to him, and that was all the explanation Richard needed.

Richard prodded at the plant. "It's not uprooted, just tilting. It'll live until Freddie gets back on Monday. What a shame." He turned to the few of them gathered there. "How are you all doing on this?"

"I think Winston here has us on the right track," said Derek. "We shall see."

Mal and Jake came running out of the garden, stopping just short of bowling over Richard. He stepped aside, laughing. "Now this is the sort of enthusiasm I was *hoping* to see from kids this weekend."

"Betty's boys are certainly enthusiastic," Derek replied.

"Yes," Richard said, nodding at the dark joke. "Aren't they, though." He was no longer comparing the brats' exuberance to himself at that age. "Excuse me, I'm going to see how the others are faring." He disappeared back into the garden.

Mal and Jake and Winston grouped themselves together on the

grass, working and reworking their map. Derek came over and contributed his own notes. Winston scribbled, erased, scribbled some more, and soon they believed they had the whole map sketched out. They brought it over to the bench where Penrose was sitting, and together the five of them stared at it.

"This is somewhat larger than your example," Derek said to Winston.

"Yeah," Winston said. "But we know we're looking for three words, and the lengths of the words will be nine, eight, and six. And I think we have to start on the E."

"The E?" Jake asked. "Why the E?"

"Do you remember? It was painted red instead of black, and had a big circle painted around it. I think that was another hint. That's the starting point."

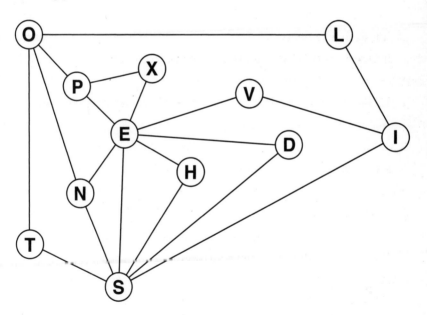

(Continue reading to see the answer to this puzzle.)

"Explosive!" Mal shouted, and again everybody jumped. "Sorry," he said, sheepish, noticing their glares. "But that's nine letters, starting with E . . ."

"You can't make the word *explosive*," Winston said, tracing it out on the map. "There's no way from the P to the L. And the only way from the O to the S is through the N."

"Well, nuts." Mal squinted again at the map.

"I like EX, anyway," said Jake.

"So do I," said Derek.

"E . . . X . . . P," said Penrose.

"EXPO?" Winston said. "Or we can go back to the E again . . . EXPE . . . EXPENSIVE!" He traced it out. "EXPENSIVE works!"

Silence fell among the group again.

"PON . . . ?" Jake said.

"POT . . . ?" Winston said.

"POLISH," said Penrose. "But no, it has to be eight letters, doesn't it?"

"POLISHED, then." Mal pointed at the map. "POLISHED is right there."

"Which paths do we still have to use?" asked Derek.

Winston made the appropriate marks on the paper. "But don't forget that a path can be used more than once."

"Never mind. I see the final word," said Jake. He traced it out. "STONES."

They all exchanged looks. "Expensive polished stones?" Mal said. "That's the answer?"

"It's a clue to the answer," said Penrose. "And the answer is six letters. So the answer must be . . ."

"Jewels," Winston whispered.

WINSTON AND MAL and Jake practically floated back to the house, delighted with themselves. They had done it! They had been the first to announce their answer to Richard, and soon they would get a prize! And from the sound of it, it would be the biggest prize so far. Jewels! What on earth was Richard about to give away? It was hard to imagine, though this did not stop Winston's mind from racing through a maze of possibilities. Mal guessed they would each get a ruby as large as a scoop of ice cream. "Here, Mom," he said, holding out the imaginary gem. "I brought a present home for you."

They gathered in the reading room, which was ablaze with the theater lighting of the mid-afternoon sun. Betty McGinley had cleaned and polished her brats, and they were back on the floor with toy cars and coloring books. Winston had to admit, they were cute kids when they were sitting still.

Winston looked out the window and saw the others walking across the lawn, chatting and enjoying the day. He was impatient to find out what they had won, which is why it looked like the other guests were walking as slowly as possible. Winston sat back in the cushiony sofa and laughed with exasperation.

"I know," Jake agreed. "Let's go already." There was nothing to do but wait. Thinking about the garden they had come from, Winston found himself jotting down the names of different flowers in his notepad, wondering if he could turn them into a quick puzzle. The answer, as always, was yes.

Each sentence below contains the name of a flower somewhere within it. For example, ROSE can be found in the sentence "The superhe<u>ro se</u>nsed danger." Can you find all the flowers?

1. Milk helps your bones grow, but I have to admit, soda is yummier.

2. Doris, Edward, and Eli, on their way to school, took a shortcut through the park.

3. After cleaning all the frying pans, your next task will be to scrub the stove.

4. Snaps, zippers, laces, or Velcro? Custom-made sneakers sure have a lot of options!

5. Once inside the cougar den, I awkwardly began taking pictures of the cubs.

(Answers, page 246.)

Penrose and Derek walked in, and neither of them looked happy. They stood in the entrance hall, and the moment Richard came through the front door, they were on top of him. "Richard, can we speak to you a moment?" Penrose asked as the other guests filed by. Looking nonplussed, Richard agreed to be led into the music room, and Derek shut the door behind them. The door was glass, and Winston could see them having a serious conversation.

Watching them, Jake said, "You know what they're talking about, right?"

"What? No. Do you?"

Jake nodded. "I'm pretty sure they think Richard's being too prize happy."

"Prize happy?" Mal said. "What's wrong with that? I like prize happy!"

"Well, some people don't," said Jake. "Like if at your next birthday, one of your relatives gave you a motorcycle. Your parents would be talking to that person pretty quick, right? Because it's too much."

"Especially since I don't know how to drive," said Mal. "You think they're trying to talk Richard out of giving away prizes?"

"Maybe," said Jake.

"Oh, come on!" said Winston. "I guess I can see why they might be concerned, but another part of me—"

Mal, nodding, finished the thought: "Wants to win some jewels!" A comic, puzzled look crossed his face. "I don't think I've ever wanted jewels before. If my parents bought me a big honking diamond for Christmas, I'd be, like, what is this? Where's that video game I asked for?"

Jake and Winston laughed. That made total sense. Winston didn't want a bunch of jewels at all, did he? He just wanted to win *something*.

The other guests were all settled in. Winston watched as Zook tried to escape upstairs, but his father summoned him back with a severe expression and a firm finger pointed at the chair next to him.

It seemed like Zook was officially on a short leash for the rest of the weekend, and possibly for the rest of his life. He was mollified only a little when Amanda made a point of sitting next to him. It was clear she had a crush, and Zook was enjoying it.

The murmur of conversation died away as Richard came into the room. He nodded to Norma, who stood up and left. Winston guessed she was going to get the jewels, whatever they would turn out to be. Penrose and Derek entered, too, and found seats. They looked a little less worried than before, so that was good.

Richard knocked on the arm of his chair to get everybody's attention. "I have been asked," he said, "to explain why I am giving away such extravagant prizes this weekend. As most of you know, at past weekend games, there were no prizes at all. Now suddenly I am giving away all sorts of things. Perhaps a couple of you wonder if I am losing my mind." He said this last with a sly smile.

Richard looked around at his guests. "It's very simple," he continued. "I realized recently that the things I have gathered over the years will one day be given away or sold. So—I thought to myself— why shouldn't I start now? And why shouldn't I have a bit of fun while I am doing it? It is a *joy* for me to give Miss Deburgh my Elgar program—" He stopped abruptly, and his face darkened for a moment, the first indication that Richard was upset by what was going on here this weekend.

Everyone in the room tried not to look at Zook, whose face was stony. Amanda wore a similar expression. She must have decided that Zook wasn't the thief after all.

"Well, assuming it turns up, that is," Richard corrected, his dark expression fading. "And my painting. I've enjoyed it for thirty years. That's long enough. I am happy to let my friend Derek enjoy it for a long time more.

"And now we have a third winner. Winners, actually—a sizable group joined forces to solve this last puzzle. Unfortunately, I have only the one item to give away, so I'm going to ask that group to nominate someone to receive the prize." He looked over to Derek and Penrose expectantly.

Derek waved his hands in a gesture of surrender and said, "I've done very well for myself this weekend. The next prize is for somebody else."

"Winston should get it," Jake said quietly. Next to him, Mal nodded.

Penrose said, "It's true. He's the one who figured out what was going on. It was his idea to make the map."

Richard looked at him. "Winston? Do you agree?"

Not entirely sure what he was agreeing to, Winston said, "Yes. I guess so."

"Excellent. Norma?"

Norma stepped forward holding a very small box. Winston had to press his lips together to fight back a laugh: Norma's role for the moment was similar to a model on a game show, the ones who stand around in pretty outfits, gesturing at shiny prizes. With her never-smiling expression and her hair pulled back into a severe bun, Norma would be the perfect game-show model in a country where a cruel dictator had banned fun.

Richard accepted the box and peeked inside. "Many years ago," he said, "I played a series of concerts in Russia. I was given a gift by the first lady. Winston Breen, I am delighted to pass this gift on to you." He held out his hand, the box resting in his palm.

Feeling something close to terror, Winston stood up, walked the three steps to Richard's chair, and accepted the little box. He felt the eyes of the room on him, and sensed the amused smiles of the adults. "Thank you," he remembered to say. He opened the box and peeked inside.

He had no idea what he was looking at. They were a pair of small discs, bulging with something that might have been diamonds—in fact, they probably *were* diamonds. Each disc was backed by some sort of clip. Winston could not imagine what a person was supposed to do with these things. His confusion must have been splashed across his face, because there was good-natured laughter at his expression.

"Earrings?" Winston guessed, knowing deep down that they couldn't be earrings. Why would the first lady of Russia give a grown man *earrings*?

Richard smiled, then laughed, then patted Winston on the shoulder with warm appreciation. "Cuff links! I believe I have given you your first set of cuff links."

This cleared up nothing.

Richard explained while Winston stood there, nodding his head and trying to look like this kind of thing happened to him every day. Cuff links were worn with certain dress shirts. Usually buttons kept the cuffs closed around your wrists, but some fancy shirts, the kind you'd wear with a tuxedo, required cuff links instead. It sounded bewildering and sort of dumb, but then Winston thought the tuxedo was the silliest outfit ever invented. His father wore one to a party some time ago, and when he emerged from his bedroom looking like an emperor penguin, Winston and Katie had been knocked over with giggles.

But the cuff links grew heavier in Winston's hand the longer Richard talked about them. Yes, they were diamonds. Not gigantic diamonds—not among the most valuable objects on earth—but diamonds nonetheless. What was more, the cuff links were antiques, passed along from some old aristocrat into the possession of the Russian first lady, and from her to Richard Overton . . . and now, finally, into the hands of a twelve-year-old boy from Glenville. It boggled the mind how things worked sometimes.

Richard congratulated him, and Winston heard the other guests applauding. Winston said thank you again, but his mind held only one thought: What was he supposed to do with these things? Forget the fact that he owned no shirt that required cuff links. When he got home, he could pop them into a drawer, and there they would stay, probably forever. What was he supposed to do with them *now*? His ratty backpack was under the sofa where he slept at night, and that was here in this room—the same room where Betty McGinley's money had been stolen. He couldn't shove these valuable things into one of the pockets, slide it back under the sofa, and hope the thief didn't go looking for them. But he also didn't want to keep them in his pocket the whole time.

Norma announced that there would be more free time. The next puzzle would be revealed after dinner.

The guests dispersed. A few people—Kimberly Schmidt among them—stopped to admire the cuff links and to compliment Winston on winning them. As Kimberly left, Winston saw Mal and Jake were snickering, so he guessed he was still turning red in her presence. She was probably used to it.

He had an idea and ran to catch up with Norma. He hadn't spoken to her one-on-one this whole weekend, and he thought she might be so sick of kids that she would bite his head off. But maybe she could help him.

She was walking through the dining room, where Gerard and Candice Deburgh were once again settling into a card game, this time with Kimberly and Derek. This group sure liked cards. As

Winston approached Norma, he realized he wasn't sure what to call her. Their host had insisted on Richard rather than Mr. Overton, but it felt awfully strange addressing Norma by her first name. And he didn't know her last name. So as he ran up to her, Winston settled on that time-tested, all-purpose substitute, "Uhh . . ."

Norma somehow understood he was calling her and turned to look at him, surprised.

Winston explained his odd predicament. "Can you keep these for me until the end of the weekend? I don't want to put them in my bag."

To Winston's surprise, she softened, even smiled. "I can see why. I'll put them back in the upstairs hall display," she said. "Be sure to remind me to give them back to you before you leave." She patted him on the shoulder.

He thanked her and ran off. Mal and Jake were gone from the reading room. Where had they gone so quickly? He walked around the hall and back into the kitchen. Off the kitchen was a whole other series of rooms—a hallway led to a small lounge with its own piano, the little brother of the grand in the main music room. Then came an exercise room, and past that, the pool.

The pool room was sort of like a greenhouse for humans—the large glass enclosure let in the sunlight and kept out the cold fall air. Assorted lounge chairs and small tables were strewn about, and in one of the chairs sat Larry Rossdale with his laptop. He didn't seem to be using it. He was frowning and staring at the sky through the greenhouse ceiling.

Larry sensed someone else was here, because he snapped out of his trance. His frown was replaced by his standard expression of clownish happiness. "Winston!" he said. "Congratulations on your victory!"

"Thanks."

"I thought I would try to get some work done," Larry said. "Trying to sketch out some mystery ideas. I'm still intrigued by the goings-on around here! I shouldn't be happy that stuff is being stolen, but I find it genuinely inspiring!"

Larry spoke with more exclamation points than any adult Winston had ever met.

"I'll tell you something," Larry continued, in a softer voice. He pointed to the chair next to him, and Winston sat. "I don't think Zook took the money. Maybe he took the Elgar program, because if not, you still have that whole locked-door problem. But the money out of Betty's handbag? I'm having problems with that."

"Why?"

"Because Chase is being more watchful of him now. Zook said he was with his father the whole time during the library puzzle, and I think that's true. I was chatting with the two of them after the puzzle had been solved. Well, chatting with Chase. Zook doesn't have a lot to say for himself. But he was there the whole time."

"So who do you think did it?" Winston asked.

Larry frowned again, however briefly. "I have a couple of ideas. They're both pretty far out there, though. The less silly notion is that Betty didn't have any money in the first place. She *thought* she did, but maybe she left it at home on the kitchen counter. I get the feeling that when her kids are around, she's a little—"

"Distracted," said Winston.

"I was going to say *insane*," Larry said with a laugh, "but your word is nicer. The problem with that theory, from the point of view of a would-be mystery writer, is that it doesn't solve the earlier crime. The Elgar program."

Winston agreed this was true.

"So for that," Larry said, "we turn to my truly wild notion. A little idea that, if I were to make it known, might get me thrown off the premises."

"What is it?"

Larry was silent for a moment, as if considering the wisdom of sharing his thoughts with a boy he had met only the previous day. But the idea was too good *not* to share—Winston could see that in Larry's gleaming, mischievous eyes—and so finally Larry leaned in and said . . .

"Norma."

Winston sat back and tried not to let his mouth hang open too wide. "You think *Norma* stole the program?" he asked in a hiss of a whisper. "And the money?"

"Maybe! Only maybe. But it makes all kinds of sense. Think about it." Larry started counting on his fingers. "She knows the house backward and forward. If anybody can get into that room and out again with the program, without waking up somebody sleeping in there, it's her."

"But why would she do it?"

"Ah! That's two," said Larry, holding up a pair of fingers. "She's worked for Richard for how long? Forever. And now what is Richard doing? He's giving away the artifacts of his career. What is Norma thinking? She's thinking, All that stuff is supposed to be mine. He has no right to give it away. So what does she do? She takes it."

Winston was boggled. Did this idea make any sense? He couldn't say—he didn't know Norma well enough to guess. But her constant state of annoyance now seemed like evidence, somehow, of what she was capable of. He thought with dismay, I just gave her my cuff links.

"But why would she steal the money from Betty's purse?" Winston asked.

Larry said, "I wondered that myself. Well, here's one possible reason: to her mind, we're all here to take away things that belong to her. We didn't know that ourselves, of course, because we didn't know Richard's plans for the weekend. But still, that's her thinking— we're here to steal from her. And so she is going to punish us by stealing from *us*." Larry considered the look on Winston's face and said, "You're not buying this."

"I don't think I am," Winston said honestly. Maybe she took the Elgar program, but stealing money out of somebody's wallet? He couldn't see it.

Larry nodded. "To tell you the truth, I'm not sure I buy it, either. I might use parts of it in my story, but I'm not sure I've cracked the mystery in real life. In a way, I hope I haven't."

"Why?"

"Because if it *is* Norma . . . well, she's going to get away with it, isn't she?"

Passing through the smaller living room on his way to find Jake and Mal, Winston spied a cabinet filled with board games. *Now* we were talking. Winston looked through them and selected an interesting one he'd never seen before. He didn't think Richard would mind.

He finally found Jake and Mal in the library—they were in there looking for *him*. They were okay with playing a game, so they spread out at one of the tables and tried to figure out the rules, which unfortunately went on for many pages.

"Holy smokes," said Mal after five minutes of reading. "Don't they have Chutes and Ladders or something? I know how to play that game."

They didn't give up, exactly, but Winston started telling his friends about the conversation he'd had with Larry Rossdale, and pretty soon the board game seemed not very important.

Jake was skeptical. "She's like the meanest schoolteacher ever, but I can't believe she'd steal from her boss."

"She's not stealing from her boss," said Mal. "She's stealing from everybody else. She knew Richard was going to give away that program, so she got to it first. Makes perfect sense to me."

"Larry's right, though—there's no way to prove it," Winston said. "Unless we want to break into the guesthouse and find all the stolen stuff."

Jake laughed mirthlessly. "Too bad I forgot my ninja costume."

They discussed it a bit more, trying to come up with some clever way of asking Norma a question so that she revealed herself as the thief. They didn't get very far on this. Through it all, Winston slid letter tiles this way and that along the tabletop.

"Okay," said Mal. "Boredom setting in. Make us a puzzle." Winston didn't need to be asked twice.

The two halves of each grid can be pushed together in two different ways—horizontally or vertically. Pushing them together horizontally creates a set of short words. A vertical push creates a set of longer words. In the smaller example seen here, a horizontal push creates HOP, COW, FLY, and ARM. A vertical push creates the words CHOP, FLOW, and ARMY.

The short (5-letter) words and long (6-letter) words are both clued in order, from top to bottom.

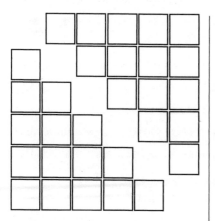

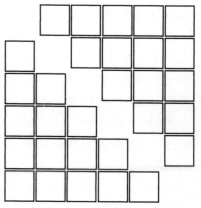

SHORTS

- Labyrinths
- Permit
- Stand still in midair, like a helicopter
- Wash away the dirt
- Button you press in some racing games for extra speed
- Object in space with a long tail

LONGS

- Astounds
- With a space at the center, like some logs
- Smart and witty
- Muslim headdress
- Awaken after being unconscious (2 words)

SHORTS

- "Bald" bird
- Small group, as of grapes
- Weapon for a knight at a joust
- No longer edible, perhaps
- Question the accuracy of
- Religious leader of a synagogue

LONGS

- Floppy-eared breed of dog
- Send up, as a rocket
- Position for a batter or a golfer
- Two-base baseball hit
- Cotton-tailed critter

(Answers, page 246.)

*　*　*

From somewhere over their heads came a sudden thump. It sounded like a book falling off a shelf and hitting the floor. But they were alone in the library. Weren't they?

They all looked up. Nobody seemed to be moving around among the shelves on the upper floor.

"Hello?" Jake called.

There was a long pause, and then some movement. Amanda came out from behind a shelf, looking embarrassed and a little angry, like it was the boys' fault she had given herself away.

"Wow, you sure like hiding," Mal said to her.

She had nothing to say to that. Gathering up her pride, she tromped down the stairs, her jaw set. She was going to weather Mal's jokes in perfect silence.

"What were you doing?" Jake asked.

"Nothing!" Amanda said. "I'm not doing anything. Just leave me alone." She made her way to the exit and left without looking back.

The boys looked up again. "Not a lot of places to hide up there," Jake said, which was true. The floor was only a couple of feet wide between the bookshelves and the railing. There were gaps between the bookcases, though, and someone truly determined to disappear for a while could squeeze herself in there.

"Maybe she's the thief," Mal said. "She's sure acting suspicious enough."

"So she stole the Elgar program she would have wound up winning?" Jake said.

"Sure," said Mal. "She didn't know she was going to win it. Maybe she paid a little nighttime visit to the Zookster and took the program when she left. She's a piano player; she knows who Elgar is. She knew it might be valuable."

Winston smiled. "The Zookster. I dare you to call him that."

"I'm sure it's his real name," said Mal. "Zook is obviously a nickname. Anyway, so she steals the thing. The next morning she solves the breakfast puzzle—sorry, Winston—and discovers she didn't have to steal the program at all. If she'd just waited, Richard would have handed it to her."

"That sort of makes sense," Jake said reluctantly.

"And what was she doing just now?" Winston asked, looking up to the second floor. "Stealing something else?"

"If she was, she hid it pretty well," said Jake. "I don't think she stuffed one of these books into her pocket."

"Don't forget she was hiding in the movie theater this morning, too," said Mal.

"Yeah. What is it with her?" said Winston.

Jake nodded in agreement. "Even if she isn't the thief, that girl is up to something."

THEY MUDDLED THEIR WAY through the complicated board game. Whenever they got to a rule they didn't understand or didn't like, they changed it or ignored it. By the time they were done, the game would have been unrecognizable to whoever invented it, but the three of them had fun for an hour, even if they couldn't figure out who had won.

They came upstairs and heard music. They ran down the hall and found most everyone gathered in the music room. Richard was at the piano, and Kimberly was sitting on a tall stool, her cello leaning against her, the bow sawing gently back and forth across the strings.

Winston had no idea what they were playing but was staggered by how it sounded.

Winston had been to a few classical music concerts over the years, dragged by teachers anxious to expose their students to the arts. Mostly he'd been bored. The music had been nice enough—*beautiful*, as his teachers rapturously described it—but after half an hour, he was done. Unfortunately, the concerts were never that short. He usually stared off into space and thought of puzzles involving musical instruments.

But this was different! For one thing, the musicians were fifteen feet away from him, not stick figures on a distant stage. He could see Richard's facial muscles tense and relax as he concentrated on a particular passage. He could see that Kimberly kept her eyes closed almost the whole time, and even when she opened them briefly, she looked like somebody having a pleasant dream.

And there was something about there being just two instruments, a piano and a cello. Of *course* a full orchestra with five million instruments is going to make spectacular music. After the first couple of pieces, it doesn't even seem all that impressive anymore. If there are only two instruments, Winston supposed, they had to work a lot harder. Richard and Kimberly didn't appear to be *working*, though—they made it look easy. The music flowing out of their instruments seemed somehow magical. It was crystal clear, like you could see the actual sound waves spreading out into the world. Winston could have sat there all day.

After Richard and Kimberly played their final notes, there was a moment of silence that ended when Mal said in a low voice, "Wow." His sincere amazement made everyone laugh and turn to see who had spoken. Mal always liked making people laugh, but usually he did it on purpose. This time he hadn't meant to, and he turned bright red.

Richard and Kimberly thanked them all. "Especially you, Mal," Richard said, with a dry smile. There was more laughter, and then the two musicians launched into another piece, exactly as Winston had hoped. Throughout the entire concert, he didn't think about puzzles at all . . . although a puzzle idea did occur to him later.

The letters in the names of each musical instrument below can be placed into one set of blanks, to make a word that matches one of the given clues. The letters of each instrument will NOT be written out in order—you'll have to do some scrambling to get your answers.

BANJO   **GONG**   **ORGAN**   **TUBA**

DRUM   **HARP**   **PIANO**   **VIOLA**

___ ___ ___ **BE** ___

Not as smart

C ___ ___ **T** ___ ___ ___

Words under a picture, as in a newspaper

___ **U** ___ ___ **-H** ___

Really enthusiastic

___ ___ ___ ___ ___ **LA**

Ingredient in many cereal bars

O ___ ___ ___ ___ **N**

Child like Oliver Twist or Annie

___ ___ **W** ___ ___ ___ **E**

The chin part of a skull

R ___ ___ ___ ___ ___ **I**

Italian food often stuffed with cheese

___ **E** ___ ___ ___ **Y**

Attractiveness

(Answers, pages 246–247.)

Dinner was another team effort. Vera the cook had stocked many jars of her homemade tomato sauce to go over pasta, but that wasn't good enough for Larry Rossdale, who insisted he wanted to make fresh. A chef had recently appeared on his television show and taught him how to prepare a sauce that would make them all die of joy. Everybody was fine with this, so he and Derek Bibb went off to town to buy ingredients. When they returned, volunteers were sought to help with the preparations. "We bought makings for an excellent salad, too," said Larry. "We're going to need every knife in the house to chop this stuff."

Winston didn't have anything else to do, so he stepped forward, and so did Mal and Jake. They were put at a large butcher block and given a ton of vegetables to chop. Others stood at the countertops, washing mushrooms or chopping onions. Larry set about slicing individual spinach leaves with the concentration of a surgeon.

Gerard Deburgh wasn't doing much of anything. He spied his daughter standing across the room and said, "Amanda, why don't you entertain everyone while we're working? Play some music for us." He gestured to the smaller piano in the room off the kitchen.

"Oh, I'd love to hear you play," said Kimberly Schmidt encouragingly.

Amanda looked horrified. Her mother saw this and came to the rescue. "Gerard, we discussed this before we came—"

"Oh, I know that," Gerard said, waving his hands and dismissing that long ago discussion.

"And you agreed she wouldn't have to play for anyone while we're here."

Gerard shook his head. "Yes, I know what I said. But she's a very good pianist, and we're in the home of Richard Overton." He looked at his daughter and said it again, in case she had forgotten where she was. "Richard Overton! Here is your chance to impress one of the great living classical musicians!" The great musician himself was standing at the counter, frowning, chopping tomatoes and trying valiantly to ignore this conversation.

"I don't want to," said Amanda.

"That's okay," said Kimberly. "Another time. It's okay."

It wasn't okay with Amanda's father. "You need to assert yourself, Amanda! Step forward and show off your talent!"

"I just don't want to!" Amanda said again. Her voice had the wobbly quality of someone holding back a great deal of emotion. "And you promised you wouldn't ask!"

"Ahhhh." Gerard waved his hands again. Maybe he had more to say on the topic, but Amanda brought the conversation to a close by running out of the room. Candice glared at her husband and then followed her daughter.

For a moment the only sound in the kitchen was of people chopping. Gerard stood there looking regretful and confused. He said to the room, "She's really very good. I don't know why she's so shy about it. She certainly didn't get that from me!"

Derek said, "She'll come around in her own time, Gerard. You can't force these things."

"Her own time? She's been taking piano lessons for ten years! She practices four hours a day!"

Mal slid his chair backward as if that sentence had hit him in the chest. The kids understood this conversation did not involve them, but this was too much. "Four hours a *day*?" Mal asked. "Really?"

Gerard looked at Mal, initially with surprise and then with a teacherly frown. "That's what you have to do," he said. "If you want to be *great*, that's what you have to do. Anybody can be *good*. If you want to be the best, that requires a special effort and a special passion." Winston got the feeling Gerard often said that last bit to his daughter. He said it like he was reading it out of a book.

Larry was very happy walking around the kitchen, giving his team of assistant cooks further instructions. Winston was told to cut the mushrooms into smaller pieces. Gerard was instructed to make himself useful and put a big pot of water on to boil. "Let's put those restaurant skills to work," Larry said to him. Gerard shrugged and said fine, giving every indication this task was beneath him.

It was sort of fun, working together as a big team, and dinner was as good as Larry said it would be. They all had big platefuls of pasta along with a delicious salad. Winston had never before used the word *delicious* to describe a salad.

As dinner wound down, Richard and Norma excused themselves. "We're going to set up the final puzzle of the evening," Richard said. "I'll ask you all to stay out of the pool area for the time being."

"We'll take care of the cleanup here," Kimberly assured him.

"Of course," Derek agreed.

Winston and the boys were given the duty of clearing off the dining room table. Mal, who could be counted on to turn a job like this into a circus act, balancing as many dirty dishes as he could on one arm, instead took the job seriously: the plates and bowls were milk-white with gold trim, and Mal didn't need anyone to tell him that they were mega-expensive.

"So, the pool, huh?" said Jake as they worked.

"Hopefully not *in* the pool," said Candice Deburgh. She too was helping to clear the table, if standing and watching the boys work could be called helping.

"Come on, that'd be fun," said Mal. "It's a puzzle *and* a contest to see who can hold their breath the longest."

After some time Norma came back and told them the puzzle was ready. The group filed through the exercise room and down a short hallway to the pool. One by one, they looked around and said, "Oooh!" Beyond the glass walls, the sky was a dark purple-black. Inside, the pool was lit from within, shimmering a magical blue. More lights around the perimeter of the room gave the whole place an otherworldly glow. The eerie beauty was heightened further by a number of silver party balloons, floating about head high. They looked like a bunch of ghosts waiting patiently for introductions. Calm piano music played—jazz this time, not classical.

Richard stepped into a circle of light. "Good evening," he said. "Welcome to the day's final puzzle. And, not incidentally, dessert and coffee, which you can find on the table right over there. The desserts need no explanation. The puzzle does. Listen closely."

When he was sure everybody was listening, he said, "Around the room are two dozen balloons. Please do not pop them. Each balloon has a word or a phrase on it. Most of these balloons can be paired up, according to a rule that you must figure out. When you have discovered the rule and matched up each pair of balloons, there will be two balloons left over. The words on these final two balloons can be put together to form a clue to a five-letter word. The first person to tell me that word is, of course, the winner."

"Mommy, I want a balloon!" said Ryan or Ian loudly. His eyes were huge as he took in the place.

"After the puzzle is done, you can have *all* the balloons," said Richard. Betty winced, and Winston didn't understand why, but then the other brother shouted, "He can't have all the balloons! I want some balloons, too!" And that one started crying, and then they were both crying. Betty immediately dragged them out of the room, once again blocked from the festivities by her brats. Winston felt bad for her.

"Are we working together or in pairs or what?" asked Chase Worthington.

"You may do as you please," Richard said. "But I have only the one prize. If you work in a group, it will be up to you to determine who should receive it."

Like Derek Bibb, who now owned an oil painting and had waved off the idea of winning anything else, Winston knew he could not accept any more prizes. Indeed, he still felt awkward about those cuff links. He knew there was a good chance his parents would tell him he should not have accepted such an extravagant gift, and heaven knew what crazy prize Richard had waiting for them this time. It could be anything. Winston had a moment where he saw himself going home in a taxi . . . towing Richard's grand piano on a flatbed trailer.

"When do we start?" asked Larry.

"You already have," Richard replied. He smiled and said, "Good luck," and sat down to watch the fun.

The guests walked around slowly, looking this way and that, like Alice in a particularly strange part of Wonderland. Winston gazed at the balloons, trying to get a sense of the words on them. It was quite a random assortment. Here was the word ACORN. There was the phrase OPEN SESAME. Here was the word PRINCESS. He didn't see any words that clearly belonged together.

He found himself walking next to Jake. "What do you think?" his friend asked.

"I've got nothing."

"MONTANA and OREGON have to go together, right?"

Winston hadn't seen either of those words. It was probably time to write things down. "I guess that makes sense," he said.

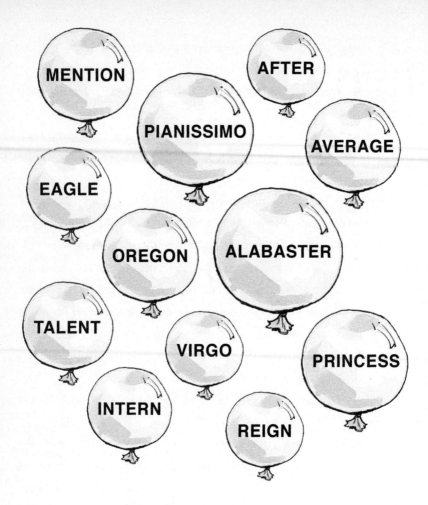

"No way," said Mal, walking up to them. "That's got to be a trick."

Jake said, "Why?"

"It's too easy!" Mal said. "Montana and Oregon? Two states? Come on. Besides, Richard said you had to figure out the rule." He held up a finger. "One rule. It's not going to be two of them are states and two of them are flavors of ice cream and two of them are things in my sock drawer."

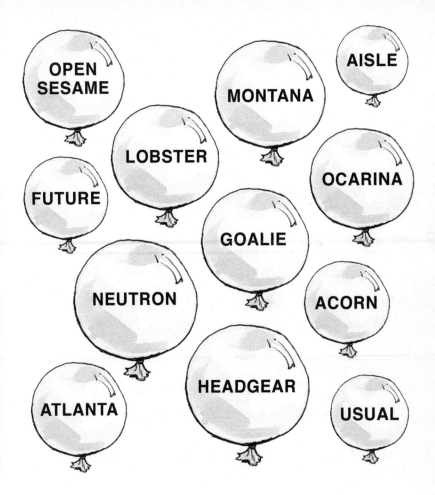

Winston looked at Mal with surprise. "Mal, you're turning into a real puzzle solver!"

"It's contagious," Mal said, "and you're like a walking germ."

"We should write these words down," Jake said. Looking around, Winston could see several people doing exactly that.

"All right," said Winston. "Let's start."

(Continue reading to see the answer to this puzzle.)

"Seriously," said Mal, looking at the list, "you have *got* to be kidding."
They had pulled together three of the lounge chairs and each was
balancing a small plate in his lap. The desserts Richard had served
were almost explosively good. Each boy was on his second helping.

Jake said, "I think Mal's right that OREGON and MONTANA don't
go together."

"Of *course* I'm right."

"I think so, too," Winston said. "I don't see two other things I can
pair up at all."

"EAGLE and LOBSTER?" Jake said. "Both animals?"

"Weak," Mal pronounced.

They stared and thought and got nowhere. That was the problem
with certain puzzles. In a crossword, you could solve a few clues,
and the letters you wrote would help you get the other answers.
Slowly, the puzzle would go from blank to solved. This puzzle wasn't
like that at all. This one was all or nothing. You either figured out
Richard's rule or you sat there staring and waiting for a big idea to
strike.

Winston looked around. The party guests had broken up into a
few small groups, as always. Penrose was at a small table with Kimberly Schmidt, who kept saying she wasn't a good puzzle solver but
who had no intention of giving up. Gerard Deburgh was, for a change,
working with his family, although it looked like Gerard was doing all
the talking and brainstorming (complete with dramatic arm-waving
gestures) while his wife and daughter looked on with expressions
that said they were used to this. Larry and Derek—clearly good
friends—were once again a team. They were still walking through
the forest of balloons, perhaps searching for some overlooked clue.
And Betty had snuck back in, without her kids, and was now

working with Chase Worthington and Zook. On the table by Betty's elbow was a baby monitor with a long, red-tipped antenna. The brats must be sleeping. Good. In fact, great.

It occurred to Winston that it would be more sociable to solve with different people, but he *liked* solving with Mal and Jake.

Not that they were solving anything.

"Where is ATLANTA?" Mal asked. "Is that in Montana or Oregon?"

"It's in Georgia, you dope," Jake said.

"Maybe there's a *different* Atlanta, in Montana or Oregon," Mal countered.

Winston and Jake gave that idea the silence it deserved. "What does a princess do?" Winston asked.

Jake said, "She sits on a throne and goes to dances and stuff. I guess. I've never met one."

"Does she REIGN?" Winston said, pointing to that word. "You know, like a king reigns?"

Mal shrugged. "Sounds okay to me. But then what?"

"I don't know," Winston said. PRINCESS and REIGN made a pretty feeble match, but it was better than any of his other ideas. None of the other words wanted to pair up at all.

Winston thought about getting a third pastry off the dessert table but decided against it. Between the pasta dinner and the two desserts he'd already had, it felt like he might not ever need to eat again. The calm lighting and calmer music—combined with his very full belly—were making him sleepy, so he got up to walk around a little, leaving Mal and Jake to continue juggling those two dozen words.

He found his way over to Penrose and Kimberly, and a smirking voice in his mind asked him which one he was here to visit. The two of them were elbow to elbow at the table, staring at the words.

Penrose greeted him. "Are you and the boys getting anywhere?"

"Nowhere fast," Winston said.

"Well, maybe we should join forces," Penrose said. "We're equally stymied, aren't we, dear?" Kimberly's reply was an exaggerated, eye-rolling look of bewilderment.

"Sure," said Winston. "I'll get Mal and Jake over here." He glanced at Penrose's notes. He had circled the letter V both times it appeared in the list. He'd also circled the letter B two times as well.

At Winston's look, Penrose explained, "Just an idea I was playing with. I'm not sure it's going anywhere. Exactly two words have a V, and exactly two words have a B."

"And only two words start with M," Kimberly added.

"Hmm," Penrose said. "That's true, too." They went back to staring.

Winston said, "Well, I'll get the others. Be right back." He walked back across the room, but slowed when he saw the LOBSTER balloon ahead of him. That was one of the two words with a B. He stared at the balloon. Some microscopic seed of an idea was trying to find a place to take root in Winston's brain.

There was a long ribbon tied to each balloon, and around the other end of the ribbon was a small weight. Winston plucked the LOBSTER balloon out of the air and held it in two hands. He gave it a little shake, as if something might be inside it. Nothing was, except for helium. Still, he felt close to figuring out something important. Whatever it was, though, it remained out of reach.

"What are you doing?" Jake asked. "Dancing with the balloon?" He and Mal had come over to see what Winston was up to.

Winston let go of the balloon. It bobbed away. "No," he said. "Let's go solve with Mr. Penrose and Kimberly." Jake and Mal immediately grinned, and Winston had to add, "They *invited* us. Come on." He turned around and strode back over to Penrose before his friends could make some new jokes about his crush (and what else could you call it?) on Kimberly.

Penrose had made only a few more marks on his paper. The Bs were still circled, and the Vs, and now he had circled the only two Fs as well. He shook his head and said, "I think I might be making notes so that I can feel smart. It doesn't feel like I'm solving anything."

"You're doing more than I am," said Kimberly.

The boys pulled up three chairs. The small table was not intended to seat five, but they managed. Jake said, "But you wouldn't expect a letter like V to be there a whole bunch of times, would you? Even B isn't that common a letter."

"That's why they're worth more points in Scrabble," Mal said.

That seed of an idea was still drifting around Winston's brain. It had neither blossomed nor blown away. "Lobster," he said.

They all looked at him. "Hungry again?" Jake asked.

Winston ignored him. "Lobster is one of the B words."

"Yes," Penrose said. He scanned the list. "And the other one is ALABASTER."

"What *is* alabaster?" asked Mal. "Is that something you eat or something you wear or what?"

"It's a kind of rock," said Kimberly. "Or a mineral, or something like that."

Penrose and Winston saw it at the same time. They both sucked in deep breaths, then looked at each other in amazement. "They go together, don't they?" Penrose asked.

"They *have* to," Winston said. They were both smiling now. The lightbulb he'd been waiting for had turned on, and it was *bright.*

The others were still in the dark. "What?" Jake asked. "Alabaster and lobster?" And as soon as he said it, Winston could see the light go on for him, too. "Ohhhh!" He jumped to his feet with the suddenness of a jack-in-the-box. "I get it!" he said.

Mal craned his neck to get a better view of the words. "If you don't tell me what you're talking about," he said, "I am going to strangle somebody."

"And I'll help," said Kimberly.

Penrose pointed to the words on his notepad. "LOBSTER and ALABASTER. They share more than a B. Look at them."

Mal and Kimberly did. Judging from the look on his face, Mal didn't expect to see anything. But after only a few seconds his eyes went wide and his jaw dropped. Kimberly was right there with him. She planted a thin finger on the paper and counted, and then laughed loudly. "I see it!"

Penrose put a hand on her arm, a signal to quiet down. Still excited, Kimberly nonetheless spoke more quietly, so as not to give the answer away to the others. "They have the same consonants. L, B, S, T, and R! In that same order!"

"Only the vowels are different," Winston said. "You take one word, change all the vowels, and you'll get a different word. That's the rule."

They bent over Penrose's notepad together, pairing up the remaining words, keeping in mind that two words would be left over when they were done.

MENTION	EAGLE
AVERAGE	OREGON
PIANISSIMO	PRINCESS
AFTER	TALENT
GOALIE	INTERN

VIRGO   *MONTANA*
OPEN SESAME   *REIGN*
LOBSTER   *AISLE*
ATLANTA   *OCARINA*
NEUTRON   *USUAL*
HEADGEAR   *ACORN*
FUTURE   *ALABASTER*

(Answer, page 247.)

"So these are the two words we have left?" Jake asked.

"Looks like it," Mal said. Penrose had circled them: PRINCESS and HEADGEAR.

"What are we supposed to do now?" Kimberly asked.

Winston said, "We put them together to make a clue. A clue to a five-letter word."

"Princess headgear," said Penrose.

"Well, that's easy," said Jake. "Crown."

"Crown," Winston agreed.

"Crown!" said Mal. "We've got it."

Kimberly chuckled and shook her head. "It's clear that none of you were ever little girls playing dress up."

Mal looked at her with surprise. "You've got *that* right."

"If you were, you'd know the answer isn't crown." She stood up and cupped her hands to her mouth. "It's TIARA!" she called.

All heads turned to see who had shouted that, and Richard was up at once, clapping his hands. "Well done!" he said. "It looks like we have our winner." There was a smattering of applause from the other guests.

Kimberly gave a graceful curtsy but said, "I only took the final step after the men here did the heavy lifting." She gestured to Penrose and the boys.

Mal waved his hands and scraped his chair backward. "Oh, hey. I'd like to win a prize and all, but I don't need a tiara. That's all yours." Winston and Jake nodded with enthusiasm. Winston was suddenly glad the "jewels" he'd won were a pair of men's cuff links. He might not ever wear them, but at least owning them would not be a mortal embarrassment. He shuddered as he imagined Richard congratulating him and handing him a sparkly tiara. Why on earth would Richard own a tiara in the first place?

"I agree with Mal," said Penrose. "The prize is yours."

She looked beyond pleased. "So am I really winning a tiara?"

"You really are," Richard said. At some point Norma must have brought it in, because Richard was holding a wide, squarish box.

"Why do you have a tiara, Richard?" Gerard asked with a laugh.

Richard smiled. "It was, of course, another gift. I have played for a lot of famous people and world leaders, and many of them feel they owe me some sort of tribute. Years ago I played a series of concerts in Sweden, including one for the royal family. The princess intended to present me with a little something, but whoever was supposed to give the gift to *her* never did. She was far more embarrassed than she needed to be, and rather than allow me to leave empty handed, she unpinned the tiara from her hair and handed it to me, along with a kiss. It was a very sweet gesture from a very gracious person. She was very beautiful as well, and now I am delighted to pass this gift on to another beautiful lady." He gestured to Kimberly, who was smiling and blushing.

"I didn't know real princesses wore tiaras," said Amanda. Winston had been thinking the same thing. Cartoon princesses, sure, but real ones?

"Oh, they most definitely do," said Richard.

"Absolutely," Kimberly agreed. She placed the tiara gently on her head. It transformed her immediately into a beauty pageant contestant. "I might never take this off," she said. She thanked Richard and gave him a kiss on the cheek.

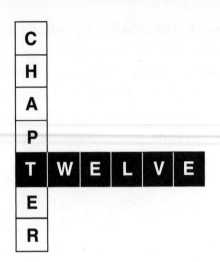

IT HAD BEEN a good day—a fun day—but it had also been very long, and Winston could feel the tiredness setting in behind his eyes. For a while, however, the entire party moved to the reading room, which is where he and Mal and Jake would eventually go to sleep. The grown-ups wanted to sit and drink coffee and tell stories. Winston sat quietly and tried to keep his eyes open, and he was grateful when Penrose talked about possibly turning in, reminding the rest of the group that they were technically sitting in the boys' bedroom.

Richard looked startled and then abashed. "Of course we are—I didn't think. My apologies." None of the boys knew what to do with this apology. This was Richard's house, after all.

That brought the evening to its official end. "There are two more puzzles tomorrow," Richard said as people began standing up and stretching. "One after breakfast, and then a final wrap-up sort of puzzle after that."

People said good night to each other and wandered off to all corners of the house. The Deburghs left to find their daughter, who was probably off hiding somewhere, and Betty went to get her sons, who were sleeping in an upstairs bedroom. Somehow she was going to have to transport them back to the guesthouse. Zook started downstairs to his room, but his father stopped him. "No," Chase said, taking Zook by the arm. He turned to Norma and said, "I'd like Zook in my room with me tonight. Do you have a cot or something we can roll in?"

"Dad!" Zook protested. His constant anger had drained away, and now he only looked wounded by his father's lack of trust.

"We do, yes," Norma said, casting a chilly smile on Zook. "Let me get that set up for you." They all went upstairs together, Zook trailing behind, glaring at the floor.

The boys slid their bags out from under various sofas and took turns in the bathroom. By the time they were done, the house had more or less closed down—Derek and Kimberly were chatting quietly in the kitchen, but that was about it. Betty had come down the stairs with one sleeping brat in her arms. The other brat was just awake enough to be led along by the hand, a child-sized zombie. Norma helped Betty drape jackets around her kids, and they all went out the front door and back to the guesthouse. When the door opened briefly, Winston could hear the wind picking up out there.

The three boys didn't talk nearly as long tonight. Jake joked that Mr. Russell, the school's music teacher, would have a heart attack when they told him where they'd been this weekend. Mal said that before they left, they would have to get a photograph of the three of them with Richard Overton. Maybe they could all pose with different musical instruments, with Richard at the piano, like they were playing a deep and important sonata.

Despite his exhaustion, sleep took a while to settle over Winston. He finally drifted off and had jumbled, confused dreams. When the thunder started rolling in the middle of the night, it woke him easily. He looked out the window as lightning lit up the sky, a gigantic flashlight flickering somewhere in the distance. It wasn't raining yet, but the deluge was sure to happen soon. He hoped tomorrow morning's puzzle wouldn't be outside, because it was going to be a muddy, sloppy mess out there.

Winston stared at the ceiling and waited for sleep to creep back over him. The world had just started fading away again when he heard a sound—footsteps? Coming down the stairs? He was instantly awake again.

Yes. A form was skulking through the entrance hall. Winston couldn't tell who it was, and he wished another bolt of lightning would illuminate the house.

For a moment, Winston thought this person was going to go out the front door. Instead, the door to the music room opened and then closed. Whoever it was turned on a light. The doors to that room had glass windows, but vellum shades had been pulled down. Against the shades Winston could see only a fuzzy silhouette walking around.

There was a lot of valuable stuff in that room, Winston thought.

He wondered if he should wake up Mal and Jake, and decided against it. He untangled himself from his blanket and stood up, a little unsteadily. There was a clock on one of the shelves—it was three forty-five A.M. Had Winston ever been awake to greet such a terrible hour?

Winston tiptoed over to the music room door. Was he about to catch the thief in action? If so, he planned on yelling loud enough to wake the house.

He put a hand on the curved brass door handle, gently pushed down, and eased the door open. Just a crack so he could see into the room.

Richard Overton was sitting at the piano, his hands splayed out on the keys. His back was to the door, and his head was bent as if in deep concentration. Winston wondered if he had been sleepwalking. Didn't sleepwalking overeaters wake up to discover themselves standing at an open refrigerator? Maybe this was sort of like that. Where else would a sleepwalking piano player end up?

Winston wasn't sure what to do. Leave him alone? See if he was okay?

He opened the door a little further. Something about the movement caught Richard's attention, and he straightened and looked around, a bit startled. He looked much older now, and he was plenty old to begin with. With his rumpled light-blue pajamas and white hair tufting this way and that, he might have been an escaped patient from a nearby hospital.

"Winston," Richard said in a creaky voice. The confusion in his eyes drained away. He had been woolgathering, in some kind of sleepless trance, but now he was back in the world. "It's okay. Come in, come in." He turned away and stared again at the piano keys.

Winston took a couple of steps into the room. "Are you all right?"

Richard thought about the question before answering. "Yes," he said slowly. "But some of the pills I take . . . sometimes I can't sleep."

"You haven't slept at all?"

There was another silence before Richard said, "I may have dozed off for a little while. Sometimes I'm not sure if I've slept or not. Isn't that funny? Norma will ask me if I've slept, and I don't always know the answer." Richard looked at him. "And what are you doing awake at such an ungodly hour?"

"I heard footsteps."

"Tch," Richard said, chiding himself. "I apologize. When I can't sleep, I often come down here to play. I can't do that now, of course.

Not with a houseful of guests. But somehow I made it all the way to my piano before I realized that. Thank goodness I came to my senses before I started in with Tchaikovsky's First Piano Concerto." He saw the blank look on Winston's face and explained, "That one gets off to a rather thunderous start."

"Oh," Winston said.

"Are you enjoying yourself this weekend?"

"I am," Winston told him. "Your puzzles are fun."

"I'm very glad you think so. And you're quite good at solving them. You're not a musician as well, are you?"

"Me?" Winston asked, surprised. "No!"

"No? Well, no matter," said Richard. "I ask because many puzzle people are musicians, and many musicians are puzzle people. Some of my favorite people are in that overlap. Wolfgang Amadeus Mozart was a puzzler of sorts, did you know that?"

Winston shook his head and shrugged. He knew Mozart was a classical composer, and that was the beginning and the end of his knowledge.

"Oh, it's true," Richard said. "Mozart once wrote a piece called 'Table Music.' It's a duet. The two musicians stand on either side of a table and play the sheet music, which is laid out between them."

Winston squinted. Something was wrong with that. "Wouldn't the music be upside down for one of them?"

Richard beamed. "Exactly! They play at the same time, and even though one of them performs it right side up and the other one upside down, it comes out sounding wonderful. Isn't that delightful? It's as much a puzzle as a piece of music."

"The musicians don't have to solve it, do they?" Winston asked. "They just have to play it."

"Of course," said Richard, waving a finger. "But don't you see, it was a puzzle for Mozart to create it. A challenge for that amazing brain of his." Richard, now looking more awake, regarded Winston for a moment and then said lightly, "Arthur mentioned to me that you are considering giving up puzzles."

"He did?" Word traveled fast in this house.

Richard said with some concern, "I hope it was nothing this weekend that made you think such a thing."

Winston looked up, surprised. "Oh—no!" he said. He considered whether or not to say anything more. "I got in trouble in school," he said.

"For solving puzzles?" Richard said, with a bewildered smile. "That hardly seems like—"

"During class."

"Ah." Richard leaned back. "Teachers do like to be the center of attention, don't they? I had problems with that myself, once upon a time."

Winston added, "And I . . . sort of broke some school equipment."

That questioning smile returned. "This sounds like a very interesting story," Richard said.

So Winston told him everything—about shattering the beakers in science lab, his notes home from his history teacher, his parents' increasing frustration, and finally the missed day at Adventureland. It occurred to him that these problems must have sounded ridiculous to a man like Richard Overton, who was famous for traveling the world and playing music for millions of people. But he listened quietly to Winston's tale, interrupting only to ask the occasional question.

Richard seemed to consider it all very seriously. He frowned and stared at the piano keys. Winston was surprised and a little uneasy that his story inspired this much contemplation.

After some time, Richard said, "Let me tell you what I think."

And at that moment, incredibly, the door opened again. Richard and Winston turned to look as Amanda stuck her head in. She was holding a glass of milk, and she looked surprised and a little lost. "I couldn't sleep," she said.

"There's a lot of that going around," said Richard, smiling. "Come join us."

Amanda stepped into the room. "I thought I heard voices, so I . . ." She trailed off.

"It's fine," said Richard. "Winston and I were just chatting about puzzles."

Winston and Amanda regarded each other. At their first meeting, they had agreed—silently but immediately—that they were from different planets and could never be friends. But now they might have been brother and sister: They were dressed almost exactly alike in dark blue sweatpants with loose, white T-shirts, each displaying a school logo. They weren't advertising the same schools, and Winston's sweatpants had a hole in the knee, while Amanda's looked like they had just been taken off a hanger. But still, it was kind of strange.

"Puzzles," Amanda repeated. She said to Winston, "Do you really do puzzles, like, all day?"

Feeling defensive, Winston said, "Not *all day* . . ."

"How long then?"

Winston blinked. "How long what?"

"How many hours a day do you do puzzles?"

She seemed genuinely curious, though she was probably making fun of him on some level, too. Winston had to admit it was a pretty good question. Between solving them and creating them, it was a *lot* of time, wasn't it? That was the basic reason why he was so troubled. So how many hours were we talking? In the morning over breakfast . . . between classes (and, let's face it, during) . . . after school and after his homework . . . maybe solving one more puzzle before bed or playing some fun new puzzle game online . . . Boy, it really added up. "I don't know," he said, unable to get a real total. "Four hours a day? Five?"

Her jaw dropped. "You sit around solving puzzles four hours a day?"

Before Winston could defend himself, Richard interrupted in a calm voice. "How many hours a day do you play piano?"

Amanda raised her eyebrows. "That's totally different."

Richard shrugged. "But what's the answer?"

She looked like she had caught herself in some kind of trap. Unwillingly, she said, "Four hours. Maybe more. But that's totally different!"

"It's not different at all," Richard said. "You have a passion for music and spend a great deal of time learning about it and practicing. Winston has a passion for puzzles." He shook his head. "No difference."

Amanda squinted and frowned, like she wanted to say there was *too* a difference, but she couldn't put her finger on what it was, not at four o'clock in the morning.

Richard continued. "Winston and I were just talking about how he's thinking about giving up puzzles. I was about to advise him on this when you came in. And my advice is, Winston, that you absolutely should not do that. Do you know why?"

Winston shook his head.

Richard leaned in. His expression grew very serious. He raised a finger and pointed it at Winston's chest. "Because," he said, "we owe it to ourselves to try to be great at something."

He let that pronouncement settle over them for a moment and

then continued. "And you can only become great at something that you love more than anything. Because becoming great at something takes work. There are many musicians out there who can play a few nice tunes on the piano, and there are many people out there who enjoy a puzzle or two now and then. But becoming *great* . . . that is a whole other thing."

Amanda had figured out her problem. She blurted out, "But a great piano player can play concerts! Make albums!"

"Make money, you mean," Richard said.

"Well . . . yeah," Amanda agreed.

"Would you play the piano if you couldn't make a dime from it?" Richard asked. "Would you play even if you didn't receive a single ounce of fame?"

Amanda looked shocked at the idea of it. It was clear she had never thought about this possibility.

Richard said, "I didn't know I was going to be famous when I started playing the piano. I was only a child. I knew I loved music, and I wanted to be great at it. I've met a lot of people over the years who are brilliant at a variety of things. Drawing portraits. Tap dancing. Sleight of hand. Not all of them are rich, and hardly any of them are well known, but every one of them is happy. Well, mostly happy. They have all become masters at something they love to do. That is all I can wish for both of you: that you find something to fill your life that makes you happy."

He looked at Winston. "For you, it's puzzles?"

Winston nodded slowly. Of course it was. He could never give it up. Had he really thought otherwise? Even for a moment?

Richard looked at Amanda. "And for you it's piano?"

There was a brief moment where Winston wasn't sure what her

answer would be, but then Amanda also nodded, though it was a slight, almost invisible gesture.

Richard smiled and clapped his hands together, a surprisingly loud sound in the dim and quiet music room. "Then bravo to you both. You don't even know how lucky you are. Some people look their whole lives for something that fulfills them, and here you've both found it so young. I'm more pleased for you than I can say."

Winston said, "But . . ." He wasn't sure what his objection was, but there was still something unsettled about all of this.

Richard knew what Winston wanted to say: "But what about your trouble in school? What about missing out on doing things with your friends?"

Surprisingly, it was Amanda who said, "Yes. Doing things with my friends. I never get to see them."

Winston nodded in agreement.

Richard nodded as well. "It's the paradox of the world. Mastering a talent can take all your time. You have to focus. You have to close out the world and concentrate only on the skill you are developing. I imagine, Amanda, that you hear that from your parents from time to time."

"My dad," Amanda said. "Every day."

"Well," said Richard, "far be it from me to contradict your father, who is a good man." He smiled conspiratorially. "But I'm going to anyway. The people who tell you to close out the world are wrong. Whatever your passion is—even if you're great at it—*it can't be the only thing you do*. You can't just lock yourself in a room and study chess your entire life. If you do, you'll be great at that one thing . . . and bad at everything else." His expression grew reflective. "Getting that balance is not easy, as you have discovered, Winston. But you have to find it. Make sure you keep your friends. And make sure you keep your head. I learned these things the hard way, over many years."

"You lost your head?" Winston asked.

Richard smiled sadly and said, "I did. I thought if I was good at piano—*great* at piano—that was all that mattered. Because I knew how to play beautiful music, I thought I was allowed to be rude and selfish and callous. . . . I hurt quite a few people over the years." He looked out the dark windows, where the storm was still churning. "There's an award that classical musicians give each other. That honor eventually fell to me, and I almost didn't accept it, even though I'd worked my entire life toward that moment. By that time, I had realized that making pretty music wasn't everything . . . and I was ashamed of who I was. I didn't feel like I deserved that award or any other. Some good friends persuaded me to accept it nonetheless, and I am glad they did. My acceptance speech was an apology for my bad behavior. It was a very important moment for me."

Winston and Amanda were quiet. They had accidentally tapped into a well of memories. Winston had a lot of questions—what on earth had Richard done over the years that was so bad?—but he knew better than to ask them. They stood there in silence for a few moments, and maybe it would have been longer. But that was when somebody upstairs began to scream.

CHAPTER THIRTEEN

IT WAS CANDICE DEBURGH. Amanda knew it first—
it was her mother, after all—and she was up the curved stairway in
a flash. Winston was right behind her. Richard couldn't run up the
stairs anymore, but he did his best. The worried expression on his
face said, *Oh, no. What now?*

Candice was in the hallway, her hands on either side of her face,
as if she were watching a scary movie and was preparing to cover
her eyes. Her husband was by her side clutching her shoulder. He
was standing in his boxer shorts and a thin T-shirt and nothing else.

Other doors opened, and people filed out into the hall, panicked
and disheveled, in various stages of undress. Slowest to emerge was
Penrose, who wasn't about to run out in sleepwear or unzipped pants,
as others had. He had taken the time to throw on some clothes. His
feet were in thin slippers.

"Somebody was here!" Candice was saying.

"Who?" asked Gerard. "What does that mean? Candice, calm
down!" He looked like he needed some calming down himself.

Mal and Jake crept up the stairs. Winston and his friends glanced at one another, wide-eyed, as Candice took a moment to pull herself together.

She said, "I came out to use the"—she gestured toward the bathroom—"the facilities, and I walked past this thing." She pointed to a large display case in the hallway, with windowed double doors on the front. There was another identical piece down the hallway, on the other side of the stairs. "I didn't turn on the hall light. And right here, right by this case, someone was hiding! When he saw that I saw him, he pushed past me and ran down the stairs! He knocked me down!"

"Who was it?" Larry Rossdale said with urgency.

"I don't know! I didn't see. It was just a shadow!"

"That Zook kid," said Gerard. He looked furious. "Where is he? I'm gonna break that kid's arm."

A toilet flushed, and they all turned around. Nobody had noticed that the bathroom door was closed. Now they heard whoever was in there washing up at the sink. The water turned off and the door opened. Chase Worthington came out, looking a little green.

"Chase!" said Kimberly Schmidt.

"What's going on?" he said.

"Didn't you hear Candice screaming?" Derek Bibb asked. "She woke the dead, I'm sure."

"I heard it," Chase said. "But some things can't be rushed."

Gerard stepped toward him, his face twisted with anger. "Where's your son?"

Kimberly said, "He's downstairs, isn't he?"

Chase shook his head and walked back to his bedroom, saying, "I wanted him up here with me." He opened the door and flipped on the light. "Zook, what are you doing? Get out here."

Zook emerged sleepily from the bedroom, and Chase gave him a light shove to get him moving a little faster. Zook went from sleepy to annoyed in a heartbeat.

His father said, "What were you doing in there?"

"What was I doing in my bed?" Zook asked. "At four in the morning? I was sleeping!"

"Didn't you hear the commotion out here?"

"Yeah, I heard it," Zook said. "So?"

Maybe Chase believed he couldn't be more exasperated with his son, but this turned out to not be true. His jaw fluttered open and closed for a moment before he said, "If you heard all the noise, why didn't you come out?"

Zook shrugged. "What's it have to do with me?"

Gerard advanced on Zook and shook him. "What's this have to do with you?" he barked. "What's this have to do with you? You knocked down my wife!"

"I did what? Get your hands off me!" Zook shook himself free. "I didn't do anything like that. You people!"

Derek was the first to regain his calm. He patted Gerard on his shoulder. "Actually, Gerard, didn't Candice say whoever pushed her then ran down the staircase?"

A slight dash of puzzlement mixed into Gerard's furious expression. He took a step back from Zook, and looked at his wife. His wife looked puzzled, too. She said, "Well . . . well . . . I *thought* he ran down the stairs. . . . It all happened so quickly. And the lights weren't on."

"Is anybody sleeping downstairs?" Larry asked.

"Not on the lowest level, I don't think," said Richard. "The boys— Winston and his friends—are in the reading room. But Winston and Amanda and I were in the music room just now, having a little chat."

"What about you two?" Gerard said. He was staring at Mal and Jake. His anger was now out of focus—he needed someone new to glare at.

Mal and Jake wore a similar look of shocked surprise. Whatever they thought they might find when they ran up here, it was *not* someone accusing them of assault.

Penrose made his first, quiet contribution to this weird meeting. "Gerard, I'll vouch for these boys."

"Vouch nothing," Gerard snapped back. "Answer the question. What were you two doing before all this started?"

"We were sleeping," Mal said.

"We heard the noise and ran up here," Jake added.

"They didn't do anything," said Winston. "When I got up, they were both fast asleep."

"And then you did what?" Gerard said. "Went into the music room? How do you know your friends didn't wake up while you were in there? Wake up and sneak upstairs?"

Penrose gave Richard a significant look, and Richard nodded with sympathy. "Gerard," said Richard, trying to use a gentle voice.

"Richard," said Gerard, imitating his host's mild tone. "How many of these incidents are you willing to put up with this weekend?" He returned his glare to the three boys. "Maybe we had the wrong idea the entire time. Weren't these kids in the reading room when Betty's money vanished? Maybe they've been the thieves all along!"

Jake met Gerard's angry look with one of his own and said, "We didn't steal anything."

Larry said with distant thoughtfulness, "Even if they stole Betty's money—and I'm not saying they did—I don't see how they could have also stolen the Elgar program. Not when Zook was sleeping in that room."

"Wait a second," said Kimberly. "Was anything stolen? Just now? Candice was knocked down, but was anything stolen?"

That stopped everything.

In the silence, Richard stepped over to the display case. He opened up one of its doors, frowning.

"Is it usually locked?" Larry asked.

"Yes," said Richard. He stepped back, gazing at the contents. "I can't tell if anything is missing. We don't open these things very often—" He stopped abruptly, as if realizing something.

"What is it?" said Derek.

Richard sighed and shook his head. All this chaos was finally getting to him, but he looked more sad than angry about it. He said in a thin voice, "Norma put something in here this afternoon. Now it's gone."

"She did?" Larry asked. "What?"

Winston realized it before Richard answered.

Richard said, "The cuff links. The cuff links I gave to Winston. They're gone."

"I thought we'd at least get to watch the sun rise," said Kimberly. "But I don't think we're getting much sun today."

They were all gathered in the reading room. Kimberly was looking out the front windows into the inky darkness. The thunder-and-lightning part of the weather had faded, but it was pouring down rain. It was almost as grim outside as it was here in the house.

They had spent the last hour discussing this latest crime, going over the same ground again and again. Larry had slipped back into his role as an amateur detective. When Candice was attacked, there was nobody in the basement, but five people were on the first floor: Richard, Amanda, and the three boys. If the thief really had run down the stairs after knocking over Candice, then it was reasonable to assume the thief had to be one of these people.

"Exactly my point," said Gerard. He was still focused on Mal and Jake like a laser beam, despite Penrose's repeated requests that Gerard calm down and think things through. The boys, Penrose said, had been asleep, like everybody else.

"They *say* they were asleep," Gerard said to them. "I think they should empty out their bags for us." He looked at the boys challengingly.

Jake was too tired to argue. He reached under the sofa that served as his bed and pulled out his duffel bag. "There you are," he said, offering it to Gerard. "Go right ahead."

"You can search mine, too," said Mal. He retrieved his ratty knapsack. "I didn't steal Winston's cuff links. But I did shove Kimberly's cello in there. Sorry. I probably shouldn't have done that." Kimberly and several others laughed. Gerard did not. He waved an annoyed hand at the two boys but decided not to search their bags. He didn't need to say what he was thinking, which was that even if the boys were crooks, they were probably not stupid enough to hide the loot in their bags.

Larry cleared his throat, trying to bring the attention back over to himself. He had a great throbbing brain full of theories he wanted to share. Perhaps the thief had only *pretended* to run down the stairs. Whoever it was went halfway down the stairs and then snuck back up again.

Penrose shook his head. "It seems more logical that the thief never went downstairs in the first place, and that Candice simply didn't witness things correctly." Candice herself was not with them. She had gone back to bed to rest her overwrought nerves.

"So that makes it Zook again," said Gerard. He wanted someone to blame, and he wanted it right now.

"Or maybe nothing at all was stolen," Larry said, and looked satisfied when everybody stared at him with amazement. "Maybe Norma never put the cuff links away in the first place. She said she was going to, but did anybody see her do it?"

"So you're saying *Norma* is the thief?" Kimberly said, astounded.

"Well, no . . . no," Larry said, a bit stiffly. Winston knew Larry *did* consider Norma a suspect, but maybe it was smarter not to say so. "I'm just saying she forgot to put the cuff links away, and now we all think they're stolen when they're really in her jacket pocket."

Gerard's disbelief radiated from his face like a neon sign. "And Betty's cash? Maybe she never had the money she said was stolen?"

Larry shrugged. "That's not impossible."

Gerard stood up. "And the Elgar program? Did that also not exist? Nothing has been stolen all weekend, is that your theory?"

"Well, I admit you've got me there. I don't have all the answers. . . ."

Gerard sat back down, exhausted. "You don't have any of the answers. If you don't be quiet, the next crime we're gonna discuss is your murder."

Richard was not a part of this conversation. This latest thing had pushed him too far: He was visibly upset and sat with Derek at the dining room table, quietly discussing things. Richard looked like he fervently wished that Norma were here to take charge. She was still in the guesthouse, along with Betty and the brats. All of them were probably fast asleep, unaware of this latest excitement.

Larry could have talked about the possibilities all day, but his listeners were getting less and less eager. The crime was going to stay unsolved—even Gerard understood this—and the group broke up to start the day. Winston had never changed out of his sweatpants and T-shirt, so he did this now. Only Kimberly stayed behind in the reading room, watching the rain fall in the barely there morning light.

"I wish I drank coffee," Mal said after they were dressed, envy in his voice as he watched the adults pour cup after cup.

"This is going to be a long day," Jake agreed. "Waking up at four A.M. is no fun."

Mal said, "Waking up and having that hamburger-selling ding-dong accuse us of stealing things . . . that's even *less* fun. If I wanted the cuff links, I could just steal them out of Winston's bedroom a month from now."

"I guess I better think of a good hiding spot," Winston joked. He paused as Mal and Jake frowned at him. "Right," he said. "Well, assuming I get them back." He'd been so tired and confused by all the goings-on that it hadn't really sunk in. *His* possessions had been stolen. He'd been unsure about accepting the cuff links in the first place, and never did figure out how he was supposed to explain them to his parents. Well, good news—now he wouldn't have to. That good news didn't feel particularly good.

Norma came upstairs and seemed surprised to see the house so busy. She began organizing breakfast, which meant hectoring people to start cracking eggs and heating up frying pans. In the fridge were the makings for omelets. Richard took Norma by the arm to fill her in on everything that had happened, but not before Norma put an unhappy Gerard in charge of omelet making. Larry offered to help, and Gerard accepted. "As long as you keep the mystery talk to a minimum," he said. "A minimum meaning *none.*" Larry smiled and zipped his lip.

Winston made his way back to the reading room, and his friends followed. Norma had just shouted "WHAT?" in response to what

Richard had told her, and the boys wanted to stay as far out of her way as possible.

Richard was depressed for a while, no doubt about it, but shortly after breakfast he regained his enthusiasm. "The next puzzle begins in twenty minutes," he announced cheerily to the group as they cleared the table of plates and silverware.

"You're really going to continue with this?" Candice Deburgh said. By the shocked look on her face, she seemed to feel her experience in the hallway should mean the end of all fun, forever.

"Why on earth not?" Richard said. "Twenty minutes in the reading room, please. Our setup for this one is minimal, so you can go into that room beforehand if you need to." He and Norma went downstairs, leaving the group to clean up breakfast.

They chatted among themselves, and after a little while, the doorbell rang. Jake answered it and found Betty McGinley and the brats. The rain had stopped, and the sun was trying to shoulder its way through the bullying clouds.

"I missed breakfast, didn't I?" Betty said. "The kids slept late, and I . . . I didn't want to wake them."

"We understand perfectly," said Larry, straight-faced. If this was a joke, Betty didn't get it. Mal snickered a little, though. "And nonsense about missing breakfast," Larry continued. "We still have plenty of food. I'll be happy to whip you up an omelet, and maybe some scrambled eggs for the kids?"

"Oh, you're a dream," said Betty as she squatted to get her kids' shoes off. The rain may have petered off, but the grounds were a mess, and mud on the expensive tile floors would surely put Norma in the hospital with a seizure.

While they waited for Richard and Norma to return and the brats messily ate their scrambled eggs, Candice brought Betty up to speed, explaining in hushed tones all the events she'd missed by staying in the guesthouse.

"*Another* thing missing?" Betty said. "The nerve this person has, whoever it is." Winston saw her eyes wander over to Zook, but he didn't notice—he was immersed in a graphic novel with a violent-looking cover.

"Okay!" said Richard, stepping into the room. He carried a manila folder and looked much more like his cheerful and mischievous self. "As always, you can feel free to work separately or together, but there is just the one prize to award." He opened the folder and riffled through some papers in there. "Take one, please. There's a copy for each of you."

The papers were passed around, and one finally landed in Winston's hands. It was fancy paper, cream-colored, with a mottled pattern in the background. Winston smiled as he took in the mystifying words:

4 paces west
4 paces north
2 paces east
2 paces west
4 paces north
4 paces east
8 paces southeast
8 paces northeast
6 paces east
5 paces west
4 paces south

2 *paces east*

2 *paces west*

4 *paces south*

7 *paces east*

8 *paces north*

8 *paces southeast*

8 *paces north*

10 *paces east*

4 *paces west*

8 *paces south*

(Continue reading to see the answer to this puzzle.)

"A treasure map!" said Kimberly.

"Without the map," added Larry.

"Well, this is very cute," said Gerard, "but how are we supposed to know where to start?"

Richard gave an elaborate I-know-but-I'm-not-telling shrug.

Chase piped up from the sofa, "Is everybody's copy the same?"

"Yes, indeed," Richard assured him.

The group stared at the papers. Nobody quite knew what to do. Penrose raised a hand and said, "And the answer is a word, correct?"

"It is."

"On other puzzles this weekend, you told us how many letters were in the answer."

"I did, didn't I?" Richard said. "That was very nice of me." He then fell into a pointed silence. Penrose uttered a little laugh. They would receive no such hints this time.

"Do we have to stay here?" asked Kimberly. "In this room?"

Richard shook his head. "Not at all. You have the run of the house. I'll be here, however, when one of you wishes to tell me the answer." He settled into his favorite chair, smiling at everyone's puzzlement.

No one moved for a while—everyone just stared at the words and looked around vaguely. Then people began to decide that nothing was going to get solved in here. "Does anyone happen to have a compass?" Derek asked. "Today's not a day for orienting yourself to the position of the sun."

"My phone has one," said Chase, bringing out a high-tech telephone, which looked like it did everything but make pancakes.

Winston thought about tagging along with them but decided against it. Knowing which way was west wouldn't be much help until they knew where they were supposed to start walking. And how were they supposed to know that? That seemed like the real puzzle.

Derek, Chase, and Zook moved to the front hallway, and after some hushed discussion, decided to go outside to look around. Had they figured out something?

"What do you think?" Jake asked. "I actually have a compass in my duffel bag. Should I dig it out?"

"I guess it couldn't hurt," Winston said.

"Here's my question," said Mal. "If this is some kind of pirate treasure puzzle, are we going to have to dig something up? I don't remember seeing any shovels."

"There must be something else going on." Winston watched as Larry and Kimberly, sparked by some hot idea, ran downstairs together. Aggravating. Winston felt nailed to the floor. He had no idea what to do.

Penrose came over, smiling. "You don't seem to be running off anywhere," he said to the boys.

Winston shook his head. "I don't know what this is. Do you?"

"Not yet. I'm willing to bet it's not a treasure map, though."

"Yeah, I guess I think that, too."

Trying their best to ignore the other groups—they could hear Larry shouting something with enthusiasm downstairs—they settled back down and tried to think it through.

Mal said, "So maybe it's a code or something. Each line represents a letter."

Across the room, Gerard Deburgh was again working with his family. He got snagged by what Mal said, and looked up. "A code? How would that work?"

"I haven't the foggiest idea," Mal said.

Gerard suddenly remembered that he was mad at Mal, who might or might not have knocked down his wife in a dark hallway. He gave a little *hmmph* and bent over his paper. Amanda, Winston was surprised to see, passed them a look of sympathy. So maybe she didn't believe Mal or Jake had done anything.

Jake thought about Mal's idea. "A code. So each line would be its own letter, somehow?"

Mal shrugged. "Like I said: no clue."

It wasn't the worst idea in the world, and Winston wasn't coming up with anything better. He said, "What if 'four paces west' means 'take the fourth letter of WEST'? That's T. . . ."

"Huh," said Jake. "But 'four paces north' also gives you T. . . ."

Yeah, this wasn't going to work. When they counted out the first six letters, they got TTAETT. Not very promising.

Penrose sighed. "I suppose we have to consider the notion that this is a trail and we have to figure out where it begins."

"Should we go outside?" Mal asked.

It would be a change of scenery, anyway, and they could see out the window that the sun was making a serious comeback. So they got their jackets and went outside into the October morning. They stood at the top of the stone entranceway and looked around.

"Great," said Jake. "Now what?"

"Well, we can walk while we think," Penrose said. "It's turning into a nice morning. Nicer than I thought it was going to be."

They strolled around the house, paying no mind to the wet grass licking at their shoes and ankles. Up ahead, Derek and Chase, with Zook trailing behind, had decided this puzzle must have something to do with the garden. They were standing at its entrance, staring at the list of clues, not sure what to do next. On either side of them were those tall purple orchids, now standing proud and tall again—someone had gotten them back into shape.

"Think they're on to something?" Mal asked.

"Beats me," said Winston.

"What about the front door?" Jake said. "Wouldn't that be a good place to start?"

They stopped and looked back in the direction of the front door, now around the corner and past several tall hedges.

"I suppose that could be right," said Penrose. "But here's my problem. Look at this." He pointed to a spot in the middle of the list. "The third instruction says to go two paces east, but then the next step is to move two paces west again."

"Two steps one way and then two steps back," said Jake. "So you're right back where you were in the first place. What's the point?"

"Score one for me," said Mal.

Winston stared at him. "Score one for you? What does that mean?"

"I mean, I'm right! This isn't a list of directions. It's a code! Like I said."

"So what's the answer?"

"I *still* have no idea! Doesn't mean I'm not right."

They all took deep, frustrated breaths. Either this was a code they couldn't crack, or this was a treasure map with no starting point. Neither possibility appealed to them.

"Fine," said Mal. "Maybe it's like a witch's spell."

Jake shook his head. "Now you're just saying random things, right?"

"I *mean*, maybe if you perform these steps, in this order, you'll somehow just get the answer. You take that last step and"—Mal gestured vaguely—"the answer just falls into your lap."

That idea made no sense at all, not one little bit. Winston assumed that was why Penrose started laughing. It was the most Winston had ever seen him laugh. The boys stared at him.

"He's right!" Penrose said during a brief moment when he was able to breathe. "We have to go back to the house! Mal's right."

"I am? I was sort of joking."

Penrose turned and . . . well, not *ran*, exactly, but walked briskly back to the house, patting his pockets as he did so, finally pulling out a pencil. At the front entrance was a pillar topped with a large lamp, and against this, Penrose smoothed his copy of the puzzle, blank side up.

"Read me the directions," he said.

Winston shook his own paper to straighten it against the breeze. He began to read. "Four paces west, four paces north, two paces east . . ." He looked up to see that Penrose was writing lines on the paper. The lightbulb at last went on over Winston's head. Of course! He kept reading. "Two paces west, four paces north, four paces east . . ."

"An E," Jake said. "That made an E."

Winston read the next couple of steps. "Eight paces southeast . . . eight paces northeast."

"That's a V!" said Mal.

They went through all the instructions, with Penrose carefully (if wobblingly) adding new pencil lines with every step. When Winston reached the end, they looked at what Penrose had drawn.

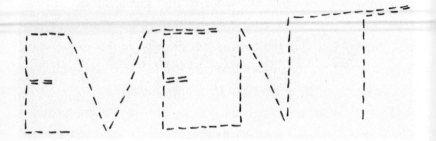

MAL RAN UP the stone stairs and through the front door. By the time Winston and the others had caught up, Richard was shaking his hand. "Well done!" Richard said. Gerard and Candice had not moved from their spot in the reading room, and Gerard was favoring Mal with a sour look.

"Thanks," Mal said to Richard. "It wasn't me, though. I'm just the runner. Mr. Penrose solved it."

"No, no," Penrose protested. "I only saw the wisdom in what Mal was saying."

Mal shook his head fervently. "I made a joke that turned out to be, uh, sort of right. But I didn't solve the puzzle. No way."

Penrose looked at him. "Are you sure?"

"I am totally sure."

Penrose smiled, and said to Richard, "Then I guess I accept whatever prize you're doling out this time."

"Excellent," said Richard. "Let's get the others in, and I'll show you what you've won."

It took a while, because Derek and Zook and Chase had to be

brought back from the farthest edge of the property. They came in, laughing at themselves and feeling a little silly. When they were all gathered in the reading room again, and after Betty's kids had been calmed down with coloring books, Richard stood up and addressed them.

"Now we're getting to it," he said. "As you know, the answer to this puzzle is EVENT. The event in question is the fiftieth anniversary of my debut performance." He shook his head with sad amusement. "This is already quite a few years ago. Time is merciless." There were regretful smiles of agreement from many of the adults.

"Anyway," Richard said, "my record company and my manager wanted to get my name out there. They wanted to hold a big celebration. I agreed, of course. I always enjoy a good party, especially if it is celebrating me. Some of you were even there, as I recall."

"I played that night," said Kimberly.

"That's right. The young up-and-comer!"

Kimberly nodded. "I was scared right out of my mind."

"The music that night was wonderful," Richard said fondly. "Everything was wonderful, in fact. The evening was held in Philadelphia, and as part of the day's festivities, I received a key to the city. I'd heard of such a thing, of course, but until then I didn't understand what it meant. I always figured some politician had a desk drawer full of keys, and every so often they'd give one to a famous visiting person. But that's not it at all." He signaled to Norma, who stood and brought over a wide wooden case.

"I'm glad to know the key is still here," said Gerard. "And not mysteriously vanished."

"Oh, it's here," Richard said. "And it turned out that the key they gave me is this beautiful, handcrafted, silver-and-bronze sculpture." He tilted the glass-topped case toward them so they could see.

Winston leaned in, and his eyes grew wide. It looked like it might open the doors to King Arthur's castle. It was enormous, and ornately and lovingly designed. This key was one of a kind, made especially for someone who was honored and admired. Just looking at it, Winston could practically hear the crowds cheering as it was handed to Richard on the steps of City Hall.

Richard held the case toward Penrose, who looked like he wanted to say a great many things. After the painting and the cuff links, Penrose had been ready to accept an extravagant prize . . . but now that it was in his hands, it seemed like too much. But Penrose also knew that if he tried to argue, he would lose. So he accepted the prize and shared a handshake with his friend. "I'm flabbergasted, Richard, really." He admired the key for a moment and then added, with frowning seriousness, "I promise not to sell this in my shop." Richard laughed and patted his friend on the back.

There'd been a break after every puzzle, so people began to wander away. Norma didn't let them wander for long before she gathered them back into the reading room. "Okay," said Richard, when they were all together again. "We are now, I am sorry to say, at our final puzzle of the weekend. It's set up and waiting for you." He looked to Norma for confirmation, and she nodded. "Are we ready?"

Everybody was ready, all right. Winston guessed that they were all thinking the same thing: So far this weekend, Richard had given away diamonds . . . paintings . . . rare memorabilia from throughout his career. What on earth would be the final prize? Winston couldn't imagine.

All he knew was he wanted to win it.

The cuff links had been stolen. Okay, it was awkward that he should have won cuff links in the first place, but for that short time, they were *his*, and then somebody in this room had taken them. Now there was something new to win. Maybe it would be something just as odd and hard to explain as diamond cuff links. That didn't matter.

Looking around, Winston could see he wasn't the only one thinking this. The final prize was bound to be the best of them all. They all wanted to win it.

Richard led them through the entrance hall and into the music room. Winston was already thinking hard, trying to get a jump on things. Maybe the final puzzle would involve Richard playing something . . . ? He hoped not. He'd be miserable at Classical Music Name That Tune.

But no, Richard walked past his piano to a door on the far side of the room. With a jolt, Winston remembered: This was where he had first encountered Norma two days ago. She'd been in there, doing something that she didn't want anybody to see. Winston had been curious at the time, but he had gotten sidetracked, first by Richard's puzzles and then by the mystery of all the stolen stuff. Now that curiosity came roaring back.

Richard unlocked the door and gestured for everybody to go in. The guests filed into a small study. There was a rolltop desk, closed like a frightened turtle, and some more music equipment, all of which had been moved to the perimeter of the room. There was only one thing in here they were supposed to look at, and at first Winston could only blink in surprise.

Two bright photographer's lights had been set up with their beams aimed at the center of the room. Sitting on the floor in this pool of light was a toy piano. Winston had become accustomed to Richard's grand piano, the centerpiece of the music room, a proud and noble thing of beauty. Seeing a toy piano in here was just plain bizarre. It wasn't even new—it might have been picked up from somebody's garage sale. It was painted a cracked and faded blue, speckled here and there with white stars. It looked a little amazed, somehow, to find itself the center of attention. One moment it had been a cast-away toy, and now here it was, lit like a celebrity on the red carpet.

Nobody understood what this could be. "So where's the puzzle?" asked Chase.

"It's right in front of you," said Richard, sounding amused. "That toy piano is the key to the weekend's final prize. Keys, actually." He looked at their bewildered faces and simply said, "Good luck. I'll be in the reading room if you want to tell me your answer."

"Wait, wait, wait!" said Gerard. "It can't just be this toy piano. Nothing else in the room is important?"

"No," said Richard. "Just the piano." He paused and said, "Well, maybe something else is important, but nothing else in the room." And with that he smiled cryptically at them one last time and with-drew to the other room to wait.

The guests all looked at each other, hoping to see a spark of an idea on somebody else's face, but right now every expression was identical: complete bafflement.

The room was barely big enough to hold them. Betty hadn't even tried to squeeze herself in. She stood in the doorway with a firm grip on both her kids—the music room was easily the most dangerous place in the house for her brats to run amok. The rest of the guests stood shoulder to shoulder, looking at the toy piano like it had just tottered down the exit ramp of an alien spaceship.

"Huh," said Larry.

"I couldn't even solve the puzzles that looked like puzzles," said Kimberly. "This is just . . . a toy piano. How is this a puzzle at all?"

"I think that's what we have to figure out," said Penrose.

Gerard was looking all around, at everything except what he'd been told to look at. "There has to be something else in here," he said. "Some other clue." He jiggled the rolltop desk, but it was locked.

Derek sighed. "Richard said *specifically* that was not so, Gerard. This little piano is the whole thing."

"That's impossible."

Derek shrugged. "Nevertheless."

"The keys," Kimberly said quietly. Everybody looked at her. "He said the piano was the key to this final puzzle, and then he said the *keys*."

"Oh!" said Larry. "He must mean the keyboard!" He knelt awkwardly at the piano. He trailed a finger up the keys, playing all of them. Frowning, he played a few jangly chords.

"Do they all play the right notes?" Kimberly suggested.

Larry quickly played every key. The piano was comically out of tune, but other than that it sounded fine. None of the notes he played sounded like a clue.

"That was a good thing to check, anyway," Larry said to Kimberly as he straightened himself up, seeming to creak as he did so. "Good thinking!"

They stared awhile. It was growing hot in this little room.

Jake muttered to Winston, "How are we supposed to get an answer out of this? There's nothing to go on! No words, no letters, no clues."

"Maybe the answer is *piano*," said Mal.

Derek laughed. "I was thinking the same thing," he said. "We're all knocking our brains out, and the answer is *piano*! Another ten minutes of staring, and I'm seriously going to try that. Because I don't understand anything else about this."

Winston didn't get it either. For the dozenth time, he leaned forward to look at the little keyboard. If there was anything puzzly about it, Winston couldn't imagine what it might be.

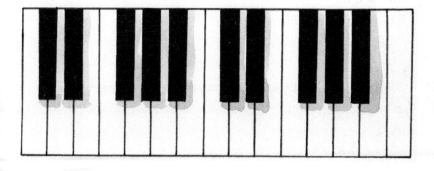

"That keyboard has to be it," Winston said. "That's the clue. Richard practically said so."

Penrose nodded. "I agree. But how do we use it?"

"All right, excuse me, please." This was Gerard, shouldering his way out of the room. His wife followed. Amanda joined her parents as they left. "I don't need to stare at this thing all day," Gerard said.

"Where are you going?" Larry asked.

"Richard said we need something else, something that's not in this room. I'm going to figure out what that is. You can all stand here if you want. I'm through with that."

After he'd gone, Kimberly said, "I guess you don't get to own a thousand restaurants without being a little competitive."

Winston scratched his forehead, trying to think. Gerard was right, actually. Richard *had* said they would need something else to solve this puzzle. But this was a big house, and Winston didn't want to comb through every inch of it looking for a clue. He didn't think that was necessary, anyway. He thought Richard was just being his usual tricky self. Everything they needed to solve the puzzle was right here in this room. And at the same time, they also needed something else. Winston could almost see what it was. A light was trying to turn itself on in his head. Right now it was dim, a flashlight with dying batteries.

They wandered away from the toy piano—staring at it wasn't helping one bit—and soon the boys found themselves at the dining room table.

"Maybe we have to play a particular song on it," Jake said.

"Why not on the real piano, then?" Winston asked. Jake didn't have an answer for that.

"Notes are letters," Mal said. "C, D, E, F, you know. Maybe we can take them and spell something."

"What's the longest word you can spell with just those letters?" Jake asked.

They thought about it. "GABBED?" said Mal.

Winston said, "How about DEFLATED?"

"What?" Jake asked. "There's no L on a keyboard. Or T."

Winston grinned. "D, E-flat, then E and D. DEFLATED." His friends groaned.

This wasn't getting them any closer to an answer, and they lapsed into silence. Chase and Zook were sitting on the stairs, studying a piece of paper. It sure seemed like Zook was seriously trying to solve this. Maybe he, too, understood that Richard had saved the best prize for last. Up above on the second floor, Gerard and Candice and Amanda stormed from one bedroom to another, looking for a clue that Winston didn't think they would ever find. They looked like people forced to play hide-and-seek for all eternity.

Kimberly was sitting at the grand piano, noodling out a little tune with one hand. Maybe she was a professional cello player, but she seemed to know the piano pretty well, too. She didn't seem to be thinking about what she was playing—the thoughtful frown on her face meant she was mulling over this final puzzle just like the rest of them.

Someone started banging on the toy piano. Winston peeked back into the small room and was unsurprised to see that it was Ryan and Ian pounding away, trying to see who could play louder. Their mother was content to let them do this: at least the boys were sitting still. Larry and Derek had been working together in that room, and they both strode away as the racket began.

Kimberly stopped playing the grand piano as soon as the kids started making noise—there was no sense trying to compete. Now she sat there frowning at the piano keys as if they were speaking a language she could not understand.

"What we need are some words," Mal said.

"What?" Winston said.

"These have all been word puzzles. Maybe this is a word puzzle, too. Except without words."

"A word puzzle without words," Jake repeated in a bored voice. "I think Mal's cracked it."

The answer came at Winston like an express train. He gasped and grabbed Mal by the shoulder. Once again, Mal had accidentally solved the puzzle. He seemed to have a knack for doing that.

"Ow!" Mal said, swatting Winston's hand away. "What's with you?"

"We need words!" Winston said in a fierce whisper. "Well, we *have* words!"

"What do you mean?"

"Something's been bothering me about the puzzle in the library," he whispered. "Remember? The answer was PURR. Why *PURR*? Why not CAT or PAINTING or something?"

"Because he needed PURR to be the answer," Jake said.

"And EVENT, too," said Mal, catching on. "I mean, he gave away a great big key. Why not make the answer KEY?"

"Right," said Winston. "He needed specific answers to make this last puzzle work."

"All right," said Jake. "So what were the answers?" He had taken out his notepad. They'd all gotten used to carrying around paper and pencil this weekend.

Winston and Mal teamed up and remembered all five answers, and gave them to Jake in order. They looked over his shoulder as he wrote.

ELGAR
PURR
JEWELS
TIARA
EVENT

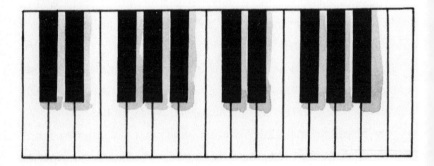

"Yes," said Winston. "That's it. I know what to do. We're almost there."

(Continue reading to see the answer to this puzzle.)

NORMA WAS TRYING to find all the guests. Simply calling out from the front hall hadn't worked, so she was going from room to room, announcing that the puzzle was over. Richard and Norma had decided to put out all the leftovers for an early lunch, and then the weekend would culminate in the awarding of the final prize. But first everybody had to be rounded up.

Winston, the winner of the prize, sat in the reading room, on the sofa he'd slept on the past couple of nights. Mal and Jake were chattering happily on either side of him. They had worked out the solution and had presented the right answer to Richard, who shook each of their hands warmly. Mal and Jake, knowing that only one of their group could get the prize, were quick to give the credit to Winston. Maybe Mal had said the thing that had gotten them going, but it took Winston to recognize it. Besides, Winston's other prize had been stolen, so it was only fair that he should get this one.

Except Winston wasn't so sure of that.

As soon as they figured out they needed the previous answers, it was a simple jump to the solution. They sketched out the keyboard and then spelled out the answer words one by one, from left to right across the keys. By placing one letter over each key, they spelled out the following:

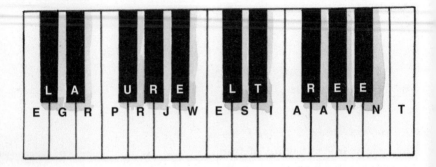

When they looked at the black keys, they saw their answer: LAUREL TREE. Jake said that sounded familiar, and Winston had to remind him: the Laurel Tree was the award that Richard had been given by all the other classical musicians.

Penrose looked stunned when he learned about the final prize. He confirmed Winston's worst fear: this was the award Richard had talked about with such respect and reverence during their middle-of-the-night chat. It was the award that meant the most to him, and now Richard was going to give it away, to some kid who couldn't play a musical scale without tying his fingers into knots. The idea of taking that award home put a heavy stone in Winston's stomach.

He didn't know what to do. He couldn't take Richard's award away—that was certain—but nobody else this weekend had been able to talk their way out of accepting prizes. The Elgar program, the painting, the cuff links . . . Richard was like a store with a sign out front: EVERYTHING MUST GO!

They had a little time while the adults got lunch together, so the boys wandered downstairs. Mal made some kind of joke, and Jake laughed, but Winston walked like he was in a daze. Maybe he could say the Laurel Tree was too fragile to survive in his house. He could say he had five little brothers, each of them as bad as Betty McGinley's brats.

They headed toward the library again. They wouldn't have access to this place much longer and wanted one last look around. A two-story underground collection of a million books wasn't something they expected to ever see again.

"So you'll take the award," Mal said. "He wants to give it away. What's the big deal?"

Jake said, "Maybe it'll get stolen before Richard has a chance to give it to you."

That was a joke . . . probably. But if Norma was the thief, Jake might also be right. Would Norma let Richard give away the most prestigious award he'd ever received?

A memory flashed by—Norma waking up Winston with her keys jangling in the front door, arriving before sunrise to get breakfast (and the breakfast puzzle) started. She had worked hard for her boss all weekend to get everything exactly right, settling for nothing less. And she'd been doing that for twenty-five years. She had scheduled his time and tended to a million little details so that he could play concerts for royalty and world leaders, the kind of people who gave him amazing gifts. Without Norma's help, Richard might never have won the Laurel Tree at all. Or anyway, that could be how Norma herself viewed the situation.

"But she can't be the thief," Winston said out loud, and Mal and Jake turned to look at him.

"Who? Norma?" Jake asked.

"Yeah," Winston said. "She wasn't here when the cuff links were stolen. She was over in the guesthouse."

"Maybe she snuck back," Mal said.

"Right," said Jake. "Through the thunderstorm."

Winston shook his head. "Even if it hadn't been raining, she would have woken us up if she'd come through the front door in the middle of the night."

Jake shrugged. "There are other doors. If she wanted to sneak in, she could take her pick."

That was true enough. Winston stood in the middle of the library, looking around for the last time. Except he wasn't really looking at anything. He was thinking too hard.

Yesterday, Norma had woken him up first thing in the morning. Today, she hadn't woken him up at all, because Winston and everybody else had been awake for hours by the time she arrived. She had shown up at her usual time, though—just before sunrise.

What was bothering Winston was that he couldn't recall Norma coming through the front door this morning. She must have, though, right? The question pricked at his brain. He had spent almost the entire morning in the reading room, right off the front hall. If Norma had come in her usual way, she would have walked right past him. Winston tried to picture the moment—the sound of Norma's keys in the lock, the door swinging open. It had been raining, so Norma would have had an umbrella. Right? Winston tried to see her stepping through the front entrance, shaking her umbrella, frowning as usual. . . . He couldn't summon up the memory.

Mal and Jake had moved to a shelf full of books about paintings, and they were each flipping through something, looking at the pictures. Winston looked at them and said, "Do you remember her coming through the front door today?"

"Who, Norma?" Mal said. "I try to stay out of her way."

Jake looked up. "Of course she came through the front door."

"You saw her do it?" Winston asked.

"Well . . . no." He thought about it. "I don't think so. But like we said. There are other ways in here."

"Yeah," said Mal. "If she didn't come in the front, maybe she came in the back. Why are we talking about this?"

Winston didn't think she came in a back door. He thought of the first time he had seen her today. She had come up the stairs from the basement, looking surprised that everybody was awake.

There was something snowballing in Winston's mind. First it was a pebble. Soon it would be an avalanche. Norma had come up the stairs! From where? There was no way into the house down here— they were completely underground. "It was pouring outside," he said out loud. "But she wasn't wet when we saw her. And I don't remember seeing any wet umbrellas anywhere, do you?"

"What?" Mal said. "Umbrellas? No, I guess I didn't see any umbrellas. But . . ."

And now an idea struck Winston—a lovely, amazing idea. It explained everything. Well, it *might* explain everything . . . maybe. Winston didn't have all the details yet. But there was one thing he was growing sure of.

He ran out of the library and down the hall. The door to the entertainment room was closed. Winston opened it without knocking. Amanda and Zook were in there, and they jumped straight to the ceiling, as if Winston had caught them kissing. This wasn't the case—they'd been sitting on opposite ends of the sofa. But still, they were not happy to be interrupted.

"Hey!" Zook yelled. "We're in here!"

Winston looked around, eyes wide, trying to figure things out.

Jake and Mal stood in the doorway, wondering what Winston was doing. They looked rather agape.

"Hello!" said Zook. "Did you hear me?"

Winston ignored this. He said to Amanda, "I know what you've been looking for."

She reared back in confusion. "What?"

"Behind the curtains in the movie theater . . . upstairs in the library. We thought you were hiding, or maybe looking for the stolen stuff. But you weren't. You were looking for something else. Right?"

"So what if I was?" She was defensive again.

"This house has a secret passage," Winston said. "Right?"

Jake and Mal looked at each other again. Their jaws could hardly be open wider.

Amanda got to her feet, also looking amazed. "How do you know about that?"

"I'll tell you in a second," Winston said. "But how do *you* know about it?"

Still surprised, Amanda shook her head. "My father told me about it. Years ago, when I was a child. He probably doesn't even remember telling me. I wanted to find it, that's all."

Winston said, "I know where it is."

Jake and Mal said, "You what?"

Zook was trying to be surly, but wonder crept into his voice. "What are you talking about? A secret passage? Come on."

Winston opened the closet. There were five shelves, used to hold sheets and blankets and pillows. It was a little emptier than usual, with so many guests in the house, but there was still some bedding left. Winston pushed it aside and knocked on the rear wall. It sounded pretty solid.

"You think that wall is a door?" Jake said.

"I don't know," Winston said. "It's got to be here somewhere."

"Why?" said Amanda. "Why does it have to be in there?"

"Because whoever stole the Elgar program came through here." Winston looked at Zook. "*You* didn't steal it, right?"

"I didn't steal anything," Zook said sullenly. "Nobody believes that, though."

Winston thought people would believe it soon enough. He'd never been so sure of anything. But that didn't mean the passage would be easy to find. He talked while he felt around. Norma didn't come in this morning through the front door. The first anybody had seen her today was when she had come up the stairs from this lower level. But there was no way into the house from here. Well, no *obvious* way.

He tried moving the shelves back and forth on their braces. They barely moved. He felt all around the closet door frame, looking for a trigger or a switch. There was nothing. "It has to be here," he said.

"If there's a secret passage," said Jake, "then it must connect the guesthouse to this house."

"Exactly," said Winston. "Norma must use it when it rains."

"So?" Mal said. "Does that make Norma the thief?"

All the attitude had been knocked out of Zook, replaced by wonder. "It has to be. She snuck in here through that door and took the Elgar program while I was sleeping! Why would she do that?"

Winston told them Larry's theory—that after twenty-five years of service, Norma saw these things as rightfully hers. She was furious that Richard was giving them away.

"So she makes me look like the thief?" Zook said. The anger was welling up again. "I'm going to go talk to my dad right now!" He started out of the room.

"No!" yelled the rest of them, and Winston said, "If we can't find the door, we can't prove anything."

"We don't even know yet that there *is* a secret door," said Jake.

"So then find it!" Zook barked at him.

Winston blew out a breath of frustration. The closet was so plain, so ordinary. It didn't look like it harbored any dark secrets. He felt around the walls again and felt only painted plaster, simple and smooth. He took a step back and stared.

It had to be here. It *had* to be.

An idea occurred to him. "Does somebody have a flashlight?" he asked.

"Yeah," said Zook. He reached into his pocket and took out a key ring. He unclipped a pocketknife, and from this he extended a stubby little flashlight. "It's not much," he said.

"Doesn't need to be. Thanks." Winston took it and walked into the closet, shutting the door behind him. He thought maybe the secret passage would open only if the closet itself was closed. He waved the flashlight around, trying to figure it out. The shelves still didn't want to move, and no magic button labeled PRESS HERE emerged on the wall. Winston was starting to think he was wrong about all of this, and he was not looking forward to admitting it to his friends.

The flashlight beam settled on something around the inside door frame. There was some kind of design—three decorative stripes raised off the wall, surrounding the door in a kind of arch. Was this "molding"? Is that what it was called? Winston thought that might be right. But why would you put decorative molding on the *inside* of the closet, where nobody could see it?

With growing excitement, he began to slide his fingers along the edge of the molding. Halfway up, he felt a small, thin break. He dug in and tried to grab this section like it was a handle. The small section of molding shifted a tiny bit—less than an inch. Winston could hear a distinct *chunk* sound. A lock unlocking. Unaware that he was holding his breath, Winston aimed the flashlight beam at the spot the sound had come from.

The side wall of the closet had opened up—just a notch, like a refrigerator that hasn't been closed all the way. Winston pushed on the wall and it opened heavily on its secret hinge. Beyond it was darkness.

Winston opened up the closet door. "I found it," he said.

CHAPTER SIXTEEN

"I'M GOING IN THERE," said Zook.

"Maybe we should tell the others we found it first," Mal said, sounding a bit dry in the throat. He was staring wide-eyed down that dark tunnel like he had seen it before in a nightmare. "We found it. Norma's the thief. The end."

"I want to see where it goes," Zook insisted. "We can't say Norma's the thief until we see that this goes to her house."

That sort of made sense, actually. But Winston said, "It *has* to go to the guesthouse, doesn't it?"

Zook shook his head. "We don't know for sure. Come on." He took a first step into the tunnel. "Are you coming?"

"I am," said Amanda. She grabbed Zook's hand. "I can't believe I'm finally looking at this. I want to see where it goes."

Winston and his friends looked at one another. Were they going to let these two go in there by themselves? How many times in his life would Winston have a chance to explore a secret passage? "We can go in a *little*," he said.

"All right," said Jake. "Just to see."

"Oh, man," said Mal. He sounded very unhappy.

So the five of them walked into the secret passage. Zook had his flashlight back, and he swung it slowly back and forth. There were also little lights strung against the walls, like white Christmas tree lights . . . but these made only a dent in the darkness. From what Winston could see, there was a single long hallway, curving gently before them. The floor and walls were cement, cracked and water-stained here and there. The smell was wet and dank.

"Maybe Mal is right," Amanda said. "We should go back." She was still holding Zook's hand and didn't look like she planned to let go under any circumstances.

"It can't go *that* far," Zook said as he walked forward. "Come on."

They walked along slowly and carefully. Winston's eyes were starting to get used to the dark now. The way the passage curved, it was impossible to tell how far they would have to walk. But surely Zook was right—this passage couldn't be *that* long. They would reach the end, turn around, and head back. Winston found he was looking forward to that. Secret underground passages lose a lot of their appeal once you're actually in one.

And then, amazingly, they came to a little intersection. The passage continued its gentle, curving arc . . . but also headed off to the left. The Christmas lights against the walls did not continue in this new direction.

"What the . . . ?" Winston said.

"I guess it goes to more than one place," Jake said.

Zook shone his flashlight down this new hallway. There were things piled up along the walls, but nobody could tell what they were. "Come on," he said, and turned down the new passage.

"Wait, where are you going?" Jake said. "You don't know which hall we want!"

Zook snorted. "What are we going to do, get lost? As soon as we get to the end of one of these hallways, we'll turn around and go back!"

"They're probably about to serve lunch up there," Mal said.

"You can go back if you want to," Zook said dismissively. He looked at Amanda, and Winston realized he was doing all this to impress her. Zook began walking down the new hallway.

"It's not even lit," Amanda said in a tiny voice. "Maybe we should stick to the other passageway."

"Come on" was all Zook said.

Winston and the others followed, but Winston started to think they were making a huge mistake. Mal thought so, too—had thought so from the very beginning—and he said, "Oh, man . . ." again. But he kept going.

"I'm not going much farther," Jake said. He had a hand out against the wall and was using it to keep himself oriented. All they had for light was Zook's pocket flashlight. Winston was trying to figure it out: If that first passage—the *main* passage—finished up at the guesthouse, then where would this one go? Winston couldn't imagine. Was there another building on the property? Someplace they hadn't seen?

The hall continued and looked like it might continue forever. The darkness seemed to press in from all sides.

Winston was about to say he was done. There was nothing down here he wanted to see. They could go back and tell the adults what they had found and let them deal with what it all meant. Maybe Norma was the thief, or maybe it was somebody else. Until he got out of this crazy little dungeon, Winston no longer cared about any of it.

Just as he opened his mouth to say something along these lines, the hallway filled with yellow light. It came from behind them.

Winston's first insane thought was that a car was coming. He whirled around and was immediately struck blind, but not before he saw somebody standing there. A large man, holding a lantern. Winston threw his arms up in front of his face, and his mind short-circuited on what was suddenly the most urgent question ever asked: Who was this man? Who could this be?

They all shouted with surprise, and Amanda's shriek rattled back and forth down the hallway.

"I guess you were looking for me," said the man. "But I found you first."

Winston squinted so he could see. The man was tall and heavily built. He was wearing dirty denim shorts that came to his knees and a T-shirt under a zip-up sweatshirt. His ruddy face was unshaven, and a thick thatch of dark hair stuck out from under his baseball cap. The man's voice sounded challenging, even threatening, but Winston saw his eyes were wide with fear.

"Who are you?" Jake asked.

"Shut up," said the man. "I'm thinking. Just be quiet."

"Are you *living* down here?" said Amanda.

The man ignored this. He turned his head this way and that like he was trying to figure out where he could go. Winston realized this man was blocking the way back to the house.

Zook realized this, too. "Hey! Let us by. You can't keep us here."

"Shut *up*," the man said. "You'll do what I say. You're not supposed to be down here!"

"*You're* not supposed to be here, either," Zook said. "I'll bet the house on that."

The man grimaced—he was trying to think, but was having a hard time of it. "All right," he said. "All right. Keep walking." He gestured down the hallway with his lantern. Winston's eyes had become adjusted to this new light source. He could see again, even if the only things to see were this scary new man and the black hallway all around them.

"No," said Zook. He let go of Amanda's hand and took a step toward the man. Jake stepped to the side to let Zook pass.

"Don't make me hurt you," said the man, a tightness in his voice. "I'll do it." But he backed up a step as he said this.

Zook saw that the man was more nervous than any of them. "You're not supposed to be here. I'm going back to tell the others." He advanced on the man, maybe intending to push him backward, maybe thinking he would just walk around him.

Whatever Zook's plan was, it didn't work. The man was not in favor of others finding out about him. "No!" he yelled, and when Zook tried to run at him, he swung his lamp, connecting with Zook's shoulder and knocking him into the wall. Amanda shrieked again, and Winston flinched as if someone had thrown a punch at him.

The man dropped the lantern—it landed on the ground with a flat *clang!*—and grabbed Zook and threw him back toward the others. Zook tried to keep his footing but failed. He tripped and fell, and rolled along the floor a few yards. He lay there, still.

"No," the man said again. "I didn't want to do that. I just . . . You can't . . ." The man didn't know what he wanted to say and quit trying. He looked around, breathing hard, his eyes wild with something like panic. He reached down and picked up his lantern. Amanda was crying. Jake and Mal were standing there, awestruck, hypnotized by this stranger. Winston wondered what was supposed to happen next. The man couldn't keep them here forever.

The man came to that same conclusion. "Okay," he said. "Get him up." He meant Zook. Jake helped him to his feet. Zook did not look anything like the authority-challenging teenager he'd been less than a minute ago.

"Get moving," the man said. He gestured down the hallway again, away from the main house. They could do nothing but agree. With the light behind them, the way ahead looked darker than ever. They had to feel their way along, with the man saying every so often, "Keep walking."

"Where are we going?" Amanda asked in a shaky voice.

"Not much farther," the man said.

This turned out to be true. They came to a ladder built into the wall. Winston could see a thin sheen of light coming through some wooden planks above them. The passage continued on, but the man told them to stop.

"Climb," said the man. "The door pushes up."

Jake was in the lead, and there was nothing else to do, so he climbed the ladder. At the top, he pushed on the wooden door with one hand. It rose up and lifted out of a square hole.

"Go," the man called to him. "And don't get cute once you're up there. Don't touch anything, do you understand?"

Jake didn't reply, but he climbed through the hole, his feet disappearing.

"You next," the man said to Amanda. She peered up, and then back at the man, her face filled with silent pleading. "It's all right," the man said. "Nobody else is getting hurt. I need to get out of here, and I can't have you in my way. Go up now."

She climbed, and then the rest of them followed. Winston went right before Zook, and as afraid as he was, he was also curious to find out where this trapdoor led. He stuck his head through the hole and looked around. Jake, Mal, and Amanda were sitting on the floor of a small, dusty building. In one corner, there were large sacks piled up—seed and fertilizer. In another corner was an air mattress, covered with a dirty sheet and a blanket. Neatly organized shelves were filled with various tools, and blocking the double doors was a large object covered with a great, dirty drop cloth. The only light was the sun coming through a couple of smallish windows. It gave the place the feel of a saloon in a Western. Winston pointed at the doors, but Jake shook his head. "Locked," he said.

Winston sat next to his friends, and Mal whispered, "It's the toolshed near the garden. Remember? It's locked from the outside with a padlock."

"Be quiet up there!" the man called from below. Zook's head emerged from the hole, then the rest of him. No sooner was Zook out of the way than the man came up. He looked around to see that his prisoners were behaving and seemed content that they were. "Good," he said. "Just sit there. Good."

"I guess you're the gardener," Winston said, and even as he said this, it seemed obvious. The purple orchids that the brats destroyed— by this morning, they had been fixed, standing as proud as ever. Who would have done that? Only one guy, and he was right here, looking around rather frantically as if he wasn't sure what was supposed to happen next. The gardener. Freddie. Hadn't Richard Overton said his gardener's name was Freddie?

Richard had sent his staff home for the weekend, but it seemed that Freddie the gardener had other ideas. He had decided to stash himself in the toolshed, for reasons Winston could not imagine. And now Winston realized that the signs of this had been there from the start. Hadn't Norma said something about missing appetizers? Winston supposed they had found their way here, and into Freddie's stomach. He had to live on something this weekend, didn't he? And the extra-warm blanket that Kimberly had wanted, which Norma had been unable to find. Winston glanced at the air mattress again. If Freddie was sleeping out here at night, and it sure seemed like he was, he would want an extra-warm blanket.

Keeping half an eye on the five kids, Freddie pawed through the tools on the various shelves. He found what he wanted—a little plastic case full of metal fasteners of some kind. He grabbed an electric screwdriver as well, and then as an afterthought he tossed three different saws down the hole. They clattered against the ground. What on earth was he doing?

Freddie picked up a small bag near his air mattress. He turned to his five prisoners and said, "Okay. Phones." None of them moved. "Phones! Hand them over. I'm sorry, I can't let you keep them. Give them now!" This last was shouted with real panic and fear, and it got Zook and Amanda moving fast. They both brought out high-tech cell phones. Freddie grabbed them and shoved them into his bag.

Winston, Jake, and Mal didn't have cell phones, and it took some convincing for Freddie to believe it. He thought every kid had a cell phone these days. But Jake stood up and offered to be searched, and maybe something about the way he said it made Freddie say, "Okay. Okay. You better not be lying." Freddie nodded like he was trying to convince himself that everything was fine.

He looked around one more time. Then he began to climb back down the hole.

"Where are you going?" Jake said, sounding alarmed.

"I gotta get out of here," Freddie said.

"You can't just leave us in here!" Amanda yelled.

Freddie said, "Someone will find you. It'll be a while. Yell, and someone will hear you. I just need time to get away." He grabbed the wooden trapdoor and pulled it over himself.

They were all on their feet instantly. Amanda tried to open a window, but there was no way to do this. She banged on it instead. "Help!" she yelled. "Hey! We're in here! Help!"

"Shut up!" Freddie called from below, sounding somewhat panicked. He was still on the ladder—he had not yet begun to run. Winston stood over the trapdoor and tried to see through the narrow wooden slats. All he could tell was that Freddie was still at the top of the ladder, doing something. There was a motorized whirring sound—Freddie was using that electric screwdriver.

"He's locking us in," Jake said. He stomped on the trapdoor in anger.

"Hey!" yelled Freddie. "Don't make me come back up there!" He continued working.

"That's why he threw the saws down there," said Mal. "So we can't cut our way out."

Winston looked out one of the windows. The lawn stretched out in front of them, and in the distance was the house. The windows of this toolshed were too small to climb through, and even if they smashed them and screamed their lungs out, nobody in the house would hear them. Not unless they were listening for it, and why would they be?

Zook tested the other walls. This place was solid and secure. It wasn't a cheap tin toolshed bought at a cut-rate department store. Freddie could have lived here forever if he didn't care about comfort. Zook punched a wall with fury. Winston saw that one elbow was scraped raw from his fall on the concrete, and his pants were ripped at the knees. Or had the pants been ripped to begin with? Winston couldn't remember. Anyway, one knee was bleeding, and now Zook spied a first-aid kit and began rooting through it.

"He's gone," Jake reported. He was standing over the trapdoor, peering down. "He's gone," he said again. He bent down and tried to lift the wooden door. It budged a little but wouldn't come up.

"We have to get out of here," Winston said.

"We can light a fire," Zook said. He was sitting on the floor treating his wounds.

Mal gawked at him. "Are you crazy?"

"What?"

Jake said, "Light a fire while we're locked in here? I want to get out of here *alive*, not charred to a crisp."

"Well, then, *you* come up with something."

Jake looked around. "Let's break the windows."

"Great," said Zook, sarcastically. "What will that do? You want to throw screws and bolts at the house?"

Amanda had squeezed her way past the whatever-it-was blocking the exit so she could push on the doors. They waggled somewhat on their hinges, but the padlock didn't allow for much more than that. She gave a panicked squawk and shoved herself against the doors repeatedly, shouting, "Hey, we're in here!" This didn't help at all, and she soon stopped.

They continued exploring the shed, trying to find anything that would help them escape. Amanda climbed back around the thing blocking the doors.

"What is that, anyway?" Mal asked her.

"I don't know," she said, and tugged on the drop cloth. It was heavier than it looked, so she dug in with two hands and dragged it away.

Underneath was a giant ride-on lawn mower.

THE LAWN MOWER was canary yellow, and Winston was surprised to see that it had headlights. Did people really mow their lawns in the dark?

Mal oohed like some impressive fireworks had just gone off, and he hopped into the seat for a closer look. The others gathered around as well, hope beginning to dawn among them.

"What do you think? Can we bust through the door with this?" Jake said.

"Oh, baby," said Mal. "The key's in the ignition and everything." He reached for it.

Zook grabbed his arm. "Don't turn that on, you idiot!"

Mal was startled. "What? Why?"

"We're in a closed-in shed. You don't want to be charred in a fire? Well, I don't want to suffocate from exhaust fumes."

Mal said in a small voice, "Oh."

Winston said, "We're going to have to turn it on if we want to get through the doors with it."

"Yeah," said Zook, looking around. "We have to get these windows open after all. Get some air in here. Even then, we better break the door down fast."

They ransacked the tool bench and finally dug up some hammers. Jake and Zook claimed them and began swinging at the windows. The panes were made of some kind of heavy plastic, and the first couple of blows did nothing at all. Zook swung his hammer like a home-run slugger with a comically small bat, bellowing pent-up rage with each blow. His window was the first to fracture into a spiderweb of cracks.

The noise of the two hammers in this small space was tremendous. Winston could tell that Zook and Jake, without saying a word, had fallen into a race to see who could break through their window first. Zook won—sharp pieces of his window flew outward. Jake battered through his window a few moments later. They stopped, breathing hard, both looking satisfied at their destructive power. Zook then started clearing away as much of the plastic windowpane as he could, making the opening as wide as possible. Jake followed suit.

"All right," said Jake, through his panting. "I think we're set."

"Yeah," said Zook. He turned to Mal, who was still sitting on the mower, and said, "Off."

Mal was offended. "What? Why do you get to do it?"

"Do you know how to drive?"

"This isn't like driving a car!" Mal said. "It's like driving a bumper car at an amusement park." But he got up, and Zook took the seat.

"We should move all this stuff away," said Amanda, pointing to the boxes and sacks that were piled behind the mower. "So you can start from as far back as possible."

That made sense, so the four of them got busy clearing a path while Zook tried to figure out the lawn mower's controls. The five of them were getting pretty dusty and gritty.

With everything taken care of, Zook started the lawn mower. The noise was horrific, louder than Winston would have dreamed. It echoed endlessly off the wooden walls like some kind of terrible sonic weapon. All of them except Zook clapped their hands over their ears. Winston hoped that the people in the house would simply hear the lawn mower and come running . . . though they would probably think the sound was coming from a neighbor's yard, not Richard's own toolshed.

Zook figured out how to stop the blade from spinning, which eased the noise somewhat. Then he shifted into reverse and awkwardly backed up. He went too far and slammed into the tool bench, knocking things to the floor. Zook gritted his teeth and changed gears. The mower jolted forward, and then began to move at a surprisingly turtlelike pace.

The mower traveled a few feet and hit the double doors. Winston had imagined Zook would smash through them, like a superhero busting into a villain's lair. That didn't happen. The padlock was too strong. The mower pushed the doors open a slight bit, and when Zook switched to yet another gear, he was able to force the doors open an inch or two farther. But that was all. The doors were too strong, and the mower was too slow to build up any real force.

Angry and frustrated, Zook threw the mower into reverse again. The doors seemed to sigh with relief as the mower backed away. Zook hit the doors a second time, but again the lock held fast.

Looking at the doors straining to stay closed, Winston had an idea. He waved his arms to get Zook's attention, then held up a hand:

Stop! Wait a minute! Zook watched, frowning, as Winston grabbed one of the hammers off the tool bench and sized it up. Yes, this might work. He signaled to Jake and yelled at him over the noise of the mower: "Find that other hammer! Or something with a handle!"

Jake gave a look like he didn't understand why Winston wanted this, but he got busy looking. Winston ran to the doors and yelled to Zook, "Push on the doors! Open them as much as you can!"

Zook nodded—perhaps he had figured out Winston's plan. He sent the mower forward, and the doors once more strained against the padlock. Winston shoved the head of the hammer into the gap between the door and the wall, just underneath the hinge, so that when Zook pulled back, the doors would not be able to close all the way. Jake saw this and his eyes lit up—*Aha! I see!* He did the same thing with the other door.

It was getting hard to breathe—the shed was filling with blue exhaust. Zook pulled the mower back, but the doors stayed wedged open slightly, like a dental patient with his jaw wired open. He got in position for another go, slamming again into the tool bench as he did so. Shifting gears, he steered the mower forward and hit the double doors right in the gap where they had separated. Both hammers fell to the floor as the doors were pushed open wider than ever. There was a sickening wood-cracking noise . . . but that was all. The doors still held.

Keeping the mower pressed against the doors, Zook yelled, "Do it again!" On either side of him, Winston and Jake scrambled to get the hammers back into position. Winston was able to fit the head in almost lengthwise this time—the doors might not have opened, but they were definitely broken.

Zook pulled back again. His eyes were shining with determination. He revved the motor and changed gears—Winston kept expecting the mower to peel out like a sports car, but again it only poked forward. But it was enough. The mower hit the doors dead center, and the left door snapped away from its lower hinge.

"Yes!" yelled Jake.

"Turn it off! Turn it off!" yelled Amanda. Zook backed away from the door, then turned off the mower. A gentle cloud of silence descended over them, and they all breathed a deep, exhaust-filled sigh of relief. Mal prodded experimentally at the broken door. The top hinge was still connected—barely—so they would have to push their way underneath like it was an oversized doggie door. But they had done it.

Jake was the first one out, crawling and grunting. He held the door open as much as he could to let the others squeeze out more easily. They stood there for a moment in the clean autumn air. The toolshed looked like a hand grenade had gone off inside it. Plexiglas shards from the windows littered the lawn, and the doors were unfixable, bent away from the door frame. The lawn mower could be seen in the wide cracks they had made, like a wild animal that had tried to escape its cage but now needed a nap.

"Come on," Zook said. They all ran back to the house.

Winston knew what they were all thinking: somehow, they still needed to catch up to Freddie.

"It's not enough to call the police," said Gerard, standing in the reading room, one fist raised but with nobody to punch. "We have to find this guy."

"He's gone, Dad," said Amanda.

"Every second counts," Gerard continued. "How far could he

have gotten? But he's getting farther away the longer we stand here talking!"

They had been standing there awhile, Winston had to admit. The five of them had burst through the front door covered in grit and grime, talking a mile a minute and all at once, so that nobody had any idea what they were saying. Even after they had calmed down a little and were able to start describing more clearly what had happened, getting the whole story out was slow going because the grown-ups kept interrupting to express their amazement.

"Wait," said Larry at one point, "you found a secret passage? You're not serious!"

"You didn't know about that?" Gerard said. "I thought everybody knew about that."

"I didn't," said Kimberly, looking astonished.

"It's true," said Richard. "I had this home built from the ground up. I thought, in my youth, that it would be clever to have secret doors. That became an underground passage connecting the main house to the guesthouse, and then also to the toolshed and the garden. They hardly ever get used anymore."

"I think they get used more often than you think," said Jake.

"Your gardener was living in the toolshed," said Amanda.

"Freddie? You're joking," Richard said.

"He *what*?" Norma said. She was livid. "He's been here the whole time? That beef-headed nitwit." She turned to Richard and said, "I *said* we should fire that guy, didn't I? After that last incident?"

"I know, I know," said Richard.

"What last incident?" Larry asked.

"We caught him stealing," said Norma. "He was ordering gardening supplies and giving them to his girlfriend's family."

"He honestly didn't know he had done anything wrong," Richard said. "He just thought he was borrowing things."

"He's an idiot," Norma insisted.

"Well, where is he now? What happened?" Derek Bibb asked.

And the adults listened, stunned, as Winston explained about coming across Freddie in the secret passage. "He locked us in the toolshed so he could get away." That was when Gerard stood up and starting clenching his fists.

At first, Richard didn't want to call the police. Winston thought that Norma was going to shake him. "He's been *living in the toolshed*," Norma shouted. "He's been sneaking around stealing things all weekend! We are calling the police." She wasn't going to argue about it any further. She stood up and marched out of the room. Richard did not try to stop her.

"Yes, of course we should call the police, but we need to do more than that," said Gerard. "We're wasting time. We have to find this guy ourselves."

"I'm sure he's miles away by now," said Chase.

Larry asked, "How long did it take to get out of the toolshed?"

The kids looked at one another. "Twenty minutes? Half an hour?" suggested Jake.

"About that," said Zook. "Somewhere in there."

"Yeah, this guy Freddie is gone," Chase said again.

Gerard set his jaw. "How far could he possibly have gotten?" he asked again. And then a new question hit him. "How did he even get out of the secret passage? Is there an exit that puts you out in the world?"

Richard nodded. "Yes. There's a ladder. It leaves you in the back of the garden."

"So he snuck out," said Derek. "He probably had a car parked nearby. He jumped into that, and he's gone."

Norma came back to hear the tail end of this. She said in a crisp voice, "Freddie James doesn't have a car."

No one knew what to say to that for several moments. Hope filled the room. Freddie didn't have a car. Was he out there walking around the neighborhood? Gerard was right: how far could this guy have gotten?

Larry stood up, in amateur detective mode again. "I want to get away from here fast," he said, "but I don't have a car. What do I do?"

"Is there a bus stop?" Jake asked.

"Not nearby," said Norma. "But outside of this neighborhood. A mile away, maybe. Perhaps a little farther."

"It's Sunday," said Candice.

"Right!" said her husband. "Do buses run on Sunday?"

Nobody had any idea. This was not a group that took a lot of public transportation. After the question had died unanswered, Winston stood up and asked Richard, "Can I use your computer?"

"Yes!" said Gerard, although it wasn't his computer to lend. "Look up the bus schedules! Good idea!"

Richard nodded. "Go ahead."

Winston ran downstairs, pursued by the others. He jumped into Richard's desk chair and got the computer going. The desktop image showed a page of sheet music, and there were about a billion program icons scattered all over this. Winston finally found a Web browser and opened it up. Norma told him the name of the bus system, and Winston typed it in.

"Why wouldn't he just hide in a neighbor's backyard?" Kimberly asked.

"A lot of the houses around here have fences," said Norma.

"Even if he did that," said Larry, "eventually he has to get out of this neighborhood."

Winston had finished clicking around the Web site. "The buses run on Sundays," he said, "but not as often."

"So he might be standing at a bus stop right now," Gerard said. He was standing directly behind Winston, both hands on the chair. Only the last shred of Gerard's good manners were keeping him from barking at Winston to type faster or get out of the way.

Winston asked for Richard's home address. He pulled up a map and zoomed in. He was starting to feel like a minor character in a spy movie. "If he went to the closest stop, and got on the first bus to pull up . . ." He studied the screen. "He might have gotten lucky—"

"Damn!" said Gerard, smacking the chair.

"And he'd be on the B18 bus. That goes all along this road." Winston traced his finger along the screen.

"Route 30," said Larry.

"He'd be here now," said Winston, pointing to a particular spot.

"We can catch up to him. We can get ahead of him," said Gerard.

"I think we should wait for the police," said his wife.

"To heck with that," said Gerard. "Print out that route. We're going to find this guy and bring him back here. Chase, you want to come with me?"

"You bet," said Chase.

"I will, too," said Zook.

"No," said Chase.

"Dad," said Zook. "You don't know what this guy looks like." And that choked off any argument Chase might have made.

Gerard grabbed the printout and ran out of the room. "Come on!"

he shouted. Winston would have sworn that on some level he was having a very good time.

Richard Overton sat in his favorite chair in the reading room. He was talking to nobody in particular. "I knew that boy had a few problems in his life," he said, astonishment all over his face. "But I had no idea the extent!" He looked around as if realizing for the first time that people were listening to him. "Freddie is an excellent gardener, you should know. He has a superb touch with plants and flowers. A real knack." He shook his head sadly.

They were waiting for Gerard, Chase, and Zook to get back. Two policemen had been here, but only briefly: After asking a few questions, they had run off, not at all happy to hear that Gerard had taken it on himself to pursue the gardener. The policemen squealed out of the driveway, intent on catching up. Winston certainly never imagined this weekend would end with a car chase.

Jake and Mal were looking out the front window, waiting to see what would happen next. Winston was sitting with them, and Penrose and Kimberly were trying to comfort Richard after this startling turn of events.

"He's been here the whole time," Richard said again. "I simply can't believe it."

"I guess we have our thief," mused Penrose.

"I suppose we do!" said Richard, shaking his head.

"Although I can't say I understand it," said Penrose. "Why would he steal the Elgar program? The cash, I can understand. And even the diamond cuff links. But why would a gardener be interested in an old music program signed by Edward Elgar?"

The question seemed to catch Richard by surprise. It hit him like a baseball pitcher's wild pitch. He looked at Penrose with bright, startled eyes.

"I was wondering the same thing," said Kimberly from her sofa. "He sure went out of his way to get ahold of that thing. Is he a big music lover? It doesn't make a lot of sense."

Richard Overton looked like he wanted to shrink back into his chair. He looked ill and suddenly very old. Winston and his friends caught one another's eye. Something was going on here.

Penrose caught it, too. "Richard? Do you know why he wanted it?"

Richard Overton gripped the arms of his chair and hoisted himself to his feet. Winston thought he was going to march out of the room, and maybe that was what Richard intended, but instead he stood there, silent. After a moment, he said quietly, "This is not what I wanted this weekend to be about."

"What do you mean?" Kimberly asked. She looked afraid.

Richard said, "I let the staff have the weekend off because I wanted this to be for friends and their families. I should have invited family members to *all* my weekend parties, not just this last one."

"Last one?" Kimberly said in a small voice.

Richard took a deep breath and decided to sit back down in his chair. He gave a little remorseful smile. "When I told the staff they wouldn't be needed this weekend, I also wanted to warn them. It was the polite thing to do."

"Warn them about what?" Kimberly asked. She already knew, though. Winston heard it in her voice.

Penrose knew, too. "You told them they might not have a job here much longer."

Richard nodded. "That's right."

"Oh, no," Kimberly said.

Winston felt a hollowed-out feeling in his stomach. He looked at his friends, and they looked similarly astounded. All three of them became statues, not daring to move. Winston remembered when his parents informed him that his grandfather—his mother's father—was very sick and might not live much longer. It was information he could not digest, a puzzle with no solution. It was like being told about a crime that would soon occur and having no way to stop it. Katie had cried at the news, but Winston hadn't. He'd been more baffled than sad. Now he was baffled again—baffled and shocked and appalled.

Penrose asked, "How long do you have?"

Richard gave a little laugh and shrugged. "Who really knows? A year, maybe. Honestly, there are some days I feel fine." He laughed again. "These past few days, you wouldn't have even guessed I was sick, would you?"

"No," Kimberly said, sounding much like Winston felt.

"So," Richard said, "I imagine our runaway gardener thought certain items in the house would be worth more money after I was gone. That's why he took the Elgar program."

The silence in the room grew heavy, but only for a minute. Mal, looking out the window shouted, "They're here! They're back!"

It was true. Gerard pulled back into the driveway . . . and he had a new passenger in his car.

If Freddie had gotten lucky, he could have arrived at the bus stop just in time to get away. But he hadn't been lucky. Gerard told them later he had thought he would have to chase that bus all the way down Route 30 . . . but as they passed the very first stop, Zook had yelled to stop the car. There was a small restaurant on that corner, and the three of them had run inside. Freddie had been in there, watching through the window. He had recognized Zook immediately, of course, but he was cornered and knew it. He didn't even try to run. When Chase told him to stand up and come along, Freddie did, sighing, like someone had done him a great wrong.

Winston found himself feeling bad for this guy. Freddie stared at the floor as he was ushered into the house and brought into the reading room. He couldn't look at Richard Overton. He was placed on a sofa, where he sat, boneless and defeated. This was not somebody with a Plan B. It was over, he was caught, and now there was nothing to do but wait and see what would happen next.

Norma went to call the police again. Larry sat next to Freddie and began to ask him questions, like the professional television host he was. Soon Freddie had spilled his whole strange story.

It turned out—to Norma's astonishment—that Freddie had been living in the guesthouse for the last couple of weeks, down in the basement, where Norma rarely ventured. He would sneak in there via the secret passage after Norma had gone to bed and shower in the morning after Norma had left for the main house. Then he would creep down the secret passage, climb out into the garden, and go straight to work.

Why on earth had Freddie done this? Freddie looked morosely at his hands as he told them. He had given up his apartment—he was behind on the rent anyway—and had moved in with his girlfriend. But then she dumped him and told him to get out. Freddie had nowhere else to go, so he slept one night in the guesthouse basement. And then one night became two nights . . . and before you knew it . . .

"All right," said Larry, waving his hand. "I get it."

When Richard had dismissed his staff for the weekend, Freddie had panicked—where was he supposed to go? Could he continue to stay in the guesthouse when there might be actual guests around? As it turned out, no. Betty McGinley wound up down there with her kids. So Freddie had retreated, miserably, to the toolshed. At least he had found an air mattress in his exploration of Norma's house.

"And then you started stealing things," Derek said.

Freddie looked at the floor. "Yeah. I needed money."

"So you took the cash out of my wallet?" Betty asked.

Freddie nodded, unable to look up.

Larry said, "But how did you get up here, to the reading room, to steal the money out of her pocketbook? Someone would have seen you!"

Winston knew the answer to that one. "He didn't steal the money here. He stole it while her pocketbook was back at the guesthouse. He came out of the secret passage, saw the pocketbook, took the money, and went back to his toolshed. Betty just didn't notice until she was here."

Again, Freddie nodded.

"And the Elgar program?" Gerard asked. "Why on earth would you have wanted that?"

"I didn't!" Freddie said. "I wanted one of the Grammy awards. I thought it might be worth something . . . you know, later." He looked up for the first time, caught Richard's eye, and looked back down. Then Freddie continued, "But when I came out through the closet, there was somebody sleeping in that room. I just grabbed something, anything, and left. I'm sorry. I don't know what's wrong with me."

"Did Richard not pay you enough?" Norma said. She looked like she might unhinge her lower jaw like a viper and swallow this doo-fus gardener in one savage gulp.

"I don't know," Freddie said. "I've never been much good with money." He sighed. After a moment, he looked up at Richard, who throughout this whole story had not said a word or asked a single question. "I was a good gardener, though, wasn't I?"

Richard allowed himself a small smile. "You were an excellent gardener." He shook his head sadly. "You're just bad at everything else."

The Elgar program was in Freddie's bag, and the cash he had stolen was in his wallet. Still missing, however, were the cuff links.

"Where are they?" Gerard barked at the gardener.

"Cuff links?" Freddie asked. "I didn't steal any cuff links!" He was wide-eyed and afraid.

"You stole them, and you assaulted my wife to do it!" Gerard looked ready to punch Freddie in the face.

Freddie did not want to be punched. He put up his hands like someone showing he is unarmed, and said, "I didn't! I didn't!"

Derek cleared his throat, interrupting the interrogation. "I have to say, I've been wondering about this. How did this gardener get from the entertainment room in the basement all the way up to the second level of the house? And then after he knocked down Ms. Deburgh, he ran back down the stairs without anyone noticing?" He looked at Freddie, sizing him up. "This is not someone I see running down-stairs quietly and gracefully, especially in the middle of the night af-ter committing a crime."

"*Someone* knocked me over," said Candice, sounding defensive. "Someone stole those cuff links!" She looked at Derek with a peeved expression.

"Someone stole the cuff links," Derek agreed. "But I don't think whoever did it ran down the stairs. Didn't Richard say he was sitting in the music room? And Winston and Amanda, too. That's practically right at the bottom of the staircase. Wouldn't one of them have heard someone running down the stairs, all in a panic?"

Winston looked up. "Hey, yeah," he said. "The music room door wasn't even closed all the way. We definitely would have heard somebody. I heard Richard *walking* down the stairs, and I think he was trying to be quiet."

"See?" said Freddie, anxious to clear himself. "It wasn't me."

"So I was wrong," said Candice with a sniff. "Whoever it was didn't go down the stairs at all. Maybe it was Zook, and he went back into his father's room."

"I think we owe Zook a number of apologies," Chase said sternly. "Not more accusations." He put a hand on his son's shoulder, and Zook looked grateful.

"Well, then . . ." Candice looked around at everybody, frowning deeply. "Well, then, I just don't know."

Derek shook his head. "It doesn't make a lot of sense. It wasn't this gardener, it wasn't anybody on the first floor, and it wasn't anybody on the second floor. It was nobody."

"It had to be *somebody*," Gerard said. He couldn't believe he still had nobody to be angry at.

"Oh, no," Winston said. The words were out of his mouth before he knew he'd said them. The puzzle-solving part of his brain had just made a terrible suggestion. All eyes turned to him. "Um," he said. He really did not want to say out loud what he'd just realized.

"What?" Gerard said. "Spit it out."

"The cuff links," Winston said. "They were antiques, right?"

"Didn't you say that, Richard?" Derek asked. And then the light went on in Derek's brain, too. He looked at Winston and said, "So you think . . ."

"Oh, no," said Kimberly. She had caught on, too.

Confusion and fury were doing battle on Gerard's frowning face. "What is going on here?" he said. "Someone just say it!"

Derek said it. "Gerard. What kind of store did your wife just open?"

"An antiques st—" He stopped abruptly and stared at his wife. He looked like somebody had slapped him.

The room was quiet for many moments. Candice stood there, furious, looking around, feeling the whole room turn against her. She was pressing her lips together so tightly that her mouth had nearly vanished.

"Mom!" Amanda yelled. "You didn't!"

Candice flailed an arm at Winston and barked, "This boy didn't need them! He didn't even want them!" She made a disgusted huffing sound and plopped herself on a sofa. "Fine. They're in my handbag."

"You blamed my son," said Chase with wonder. "You said he knocked you down!"

"I *told* you," said Zook. "I didn't steal anything."

"I made too much noise getting the lock on the case open," Candice said. "I thought someone had heard. So I . . ." She gestured lightly in the air. She didn't want to say "so I made up an entire phony crime," but everyone knew what she meant.

"Gerard," said Richard in his calmest voice. "I don't know if I will have another weekend party. But if I do . . . I think you should leave your wife at home."

The police returned, but nobody was arrested. Richard refused to allow it, to everyone's surprise and Norma's loud dismay. Freddie was escorted off the premises and driven away, into whatever woeful future awaited him. Sighing, Freddie said that he would probably wind up back at his parents' house. His father would not be happy to see him—he thought he was a complete screwup.

"His father's right," Mal muttered.

The Deburghs decided, too, that it was time to leave. While Gerard carried bag after bag out the door—no one felt particularly obliged to help him—Amanda said her good-byes. She was a lot friendlier now than she had been at the beginning of the weekend.

"I'm sorry about my mom," she said to Winston.

"It's all right," Winston said. The cuff links were back in his pocket.

"She just thinks she should have whatever she wants," Amanda said, embarrassed. Off at the front door, her father called her name in a let's-go-already tone of voice. "Anyway," she said. "Good luck with your puzzles."

"Good luck with your music."

Amanda frowned a little at that for some reason and started to walk away. Then, changing her mind, she walked briskly back and asked for Winston's notepad. She wrote down her e-mail address for him. Surprised, he wrote down his own, and handed it to her. Mal and Jake watched this exchange with puzzled interest. Amanda's father called her again, and she yelled, "All right already!" Then she was gone.

"What was that?" Mal asked.

"Dunno," Winston said, looking at the paper Amanda had handed him.

Slowly, the house returned to normal. Lunch was thrown together from the various leftovers in the fridge. Winston would soon be awarded Richard's Laurel Tree award, and Winston knew if he was going to prevent that, he had to do something quick. He looked around for Richard, but their host had vanished. Winston hoped he hadn't gone upstairs to lie down.

"Wait here, okay?" he told his friends, and he ran downstairs. He found Richard in his office, staring off into space. It had been a strange day, one that required a good deal of thought.

Winston knocked lightly on the door. Richard, startled out of his contemplation, swiveled in his chair.

"Can I come in?" Winston asked.

"Of course, of course." Richard looked around. "Pardon the mess. This is the one part of the house the housekeeper is not allowed to touch. You can see the result for yourself."

Winston smiled automatically. Richard's office, while not neat, was cleaner than Winston's bedroom.

"I'm so sorry about Freddie," Richard said. "Are you okay?" It was the thousandth time someone had asked that question today.

"I'm fine," Winston said. "Only Zook got hurt, and only a little bit. Your garden shed didn't come out of it too good, though."

Richard nodded. "So I heard. That's okay."

They both fell quiet. Winston was here for a reason, and Richard was waiting to find out what it was.

"I'm sorry," Winston said, "for, you know . . . why Freddie took the music program." No force on earth could make him say the word *dying*.

Richard smiled. "That's okay, Winston."

They were silent for a moment, and finally Winston stopped

trying to be tricky and instead blurted it out. "I can't take your Laurel Tree award. I just can't."

"But I don't need it anymore," Richard said. "In fact, in a way, I never needed it. The honor of receiving it . . . the memories of that night . . . they're much more important to me than the award itself."

"I still can't take it," Winston said again. "You should have it here. I got the cuff links back. That's enough. And the Laurel Tree . . . You told me how important it is. It would feel too strange taking it from you, after learning what we just learned." Winston wasn't about to tell him that he had been uneasy about taking the award even *before* he'd learned Richard was ill.

Richard gazed at him thoughtfully. "I'll tell you what. I'll make you a deal."

"A deal?"

"Tell me you don't plan on giving up puzzles. In fact, I'll go one better. Promise me you'll send me some puzzles. One a week. If you do that, I'll keep my Laurel Tree. For a while longer."

Winston was visibly relieved. "I'm not giving up puzzles," he said. "I'll send you as many as you want."

Richard smiled again. "I hope you enjoyed the weekend, Winston," he said. "Even if there were a few unplanned events. I am glad to have met you." He spun his chair slightly, back to his desk. "In fact," he said, "I was just sitting down to solve a puzzle out of one of my magazines. It's my usual method of escape." Winston smiled— he understood that very well. Flipping through the magazine on his desk, Richard said, "Want to help?"

So Winston sat down and pulled his chair in, and the two of them stared at the puzzle. When lunch was ready, an irritated Norma had to come down to get them. Neither of them heard her calling.

Twelve answers in this flower-shaped grid will be entered clockwise, beginning from each numbered space and curving inward to the center. The other twelve clues will be entered counterclockwise, beginning from those same spaces. Work back and forth until you have completed the grid.

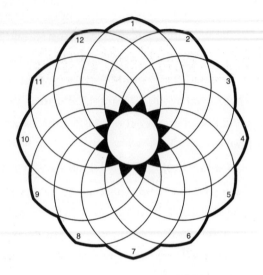

Clockwise

1. Electrical "juice"
2. Sport for cowboys
3. Cooked too much, like toast
4. Performing, as an action
5. Radiate light
6. Some army actions
7. How a lizard feels
8. Like someone from Dublin
9. "Yum!"
10. Certain "buildings" made of snow
11. Uncovered
12. Makes less difficult

Counterclockwise

1. Birthday ___
2. Red flowers
3. Bent to acknowledge applause
4. Guys, slangily
5. More achy
6. Safari animal, for short
7. Incredibly good person
8. Cake decoration
9. Swap
10. Doesn't succeed
11. Like someone who orders people around
12. Our planet

(Answer, page 247.)

EIGHT MONTHS PASSED. One moment it was a gloomy fall, with Winston drowning in homework and struggling with his grades. And then it was nearly summer again. His parents often commented on how fast time seemed to be flying. This was the first time he had felt the sensation so keenly.

Along the way, Winston had turned thirteen. He felt like he was too old for a birthday party—was he supposed to wear a pointed hat with the elastic under his chin?—but Mal and Jake worked together to make a bunch of puzzles, and they gave them to him as a present.

Winston received a couple more notes home from his boring history teacher . . . but only two over the rest of the school year, as opposed to the three he had gotten in the first few weeks. His parents didn't come down on him too hard, and his grades rose to where they were supposed to be. He saved the puzzles for downtime at school, and while life wasn't perfect—it rarely is for thirteen-year-olds—he felt more or less like someone who had gotten his act together.

Even though he remembered Amanda had taken his e-mail address, it was still a surprise when her first e-mail popped up in his in-box. Her father, furious over the stolen cuff links, had decided not to fund his wife's antiques store after all. It closed down just eight weeks after it opened. So while Candice Deburgh didn't go to jail—as Winston had thought she might at the time—she didn't entirely escape punishment.

They wrote back and forth a few times before Amanda attached a large file. Winston clicked on it and piano music filled the room.

"After our conversation with Richard in the music room, I started thinking about things," she wrote. "I'm not playing classical music for a million hours a day anymore. My father is really angry about it, but it's not what I want to do. I'm writing music instead."

Winston was amazed. She had *written* the music coming out of his computer speakers?

"I'm trying to write a song every couple of weeks," her e-mail said. "It's not easy! I think I have a lot to learn. But I'm having way more fun at the piano now. I've attached this week's song. I hope you like it."

The song had no lyrics—Winston guessed she wanted to focus only on the music—but it was a bright, lively piece. Maybe she had a lot to learn, but this sounded pretty good to him. He remembered the last time he had listened to piano music here in his bedroom. It was the CD that Penrose had given him, of Richard Overton's music.

Richard had died a few weeks earlier. He had taken a nap after lunch and simply never woke up. Winston read everything he could about it. In the news were quotes and comments from many of the people he had met that weekend. Kimberly Schmidt called him "a giant" and "a wonderful friend." Derek Bibb told a reporter about the puzzle and game parties Richard would throw. Larry Rossdale did a special segment on his television show. Winston had recorded it and watched it several times. He had sent Richard a bunch of puzzles over the last few months, and sometimes Richard would write back, saying he particularly liked one or another.

And now, on this very day, a package had arrived for Winston. It was sitting on his bed and had Norma's name on the return address. Winston thought he knew what was in it. He wasn't ready to open it up yet. Maybe a little later.

He sat there listening to Amanda's music, looking out the window at the bright sunshine. He should go outside, and in a little while, he would.

But this morning at breakfast he had started to get an idea for a puzzle . . . maybe even a whole series of puzzles. Yes. Eighth grade was almost over; next year he would be in high school. He was a little nervous about that, but that was a problem for another time. Today he had the day to himself, and a good idea was slowly blossoming in his mind. He reached for a pencil and his notebook. He wanted to get started.

THE CONTINUING ADVENTURES OF PUZZLEMAN

BY WINSTON BREEN

THERE'S ONLY ONE superhero who fights crime by solving puzzles: Puzzleman! And this time he's up against his most deadly adversary: the Shock! This bad guy harnesses the power of electricity, and nobody is safe when those lightning bolts start flying! What's more, the Shock has a crew of six other supervillains, each with their own nasty powers.

First, help Puzzleman defeat the Shock's six henchmen by solving their puzzles. Then use the information from each puzzle answer to figure out how to defeat the Shock once and for all!

The Mad Zookeeper

The Mad Zookeeper is fed up with animals! He's so angry, in fact, that he's developed the power to change animals into other objects. Luckily, your puzzling powers can restore all the animals to normal.

Part 1:

Apply each of the directions on the next page to one of the pictures seen here. The result will be an animal, which you should write in the blanks under the picture.

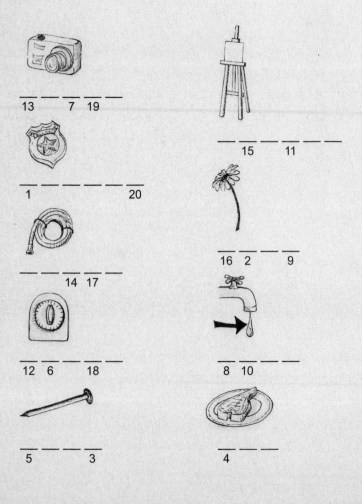

___ ___ ___ ___
13   7   19

___ ___ ___ ___ ___
1   20

___ ___ ___ ___
   14 17

___ ___ ___ ___
12 6   18

___ ___ ___
5   3

___ ___ ___ ___ ___
   15   11

___ ___ ___ ___
16 2   9

___ ___ ___ ___
8 10

___ ___ ___
4

- Add an R to the end of the object.
- Add an R somewhere in the middle of the object.
- Add a W to the start of the object.
- Replace the first three letters with a Y.
- Remove the last two letters and spell what remains backward.
- Change the second letter to an O and spell backward.
- Replace the last two letters with an L.
- Change the last letter to a B and spell backward.
- Change the third letter to a G.

* * *

Part 2:

Transfer all the numbered letters from Part 1 into the blanks below. When you're done, you'll have five words. You can change one letter in each word to give you the name of an animal. The five letters you change, reading down, will spell the answer to this puzzle.

— — — —
1   2   3   4

— — — —
5   6   7   8

— — — —
9 10 11 12

— — — —
13 14 15 16

— — — —
17 18 19 20

Switcheroo

Switcheroo does his dirty work very cleverly—he changes things so slightly that at first no one even realizes anything is wrong, much less that something has been stolen. Examine the scenes below. The first picture shows this clock shop before Switcheroo arrived; the second picture shows what it looked like after he left. Look closely

and you'll find ten differences between the pictures, one in each row from 1 to 10. Circle each change you spot, and then trace your finger upward to the letter at the top of the picture. Write that letter in the appropriately numbered blanks as many times as necessary. When you're done, you'll spell out a clue.

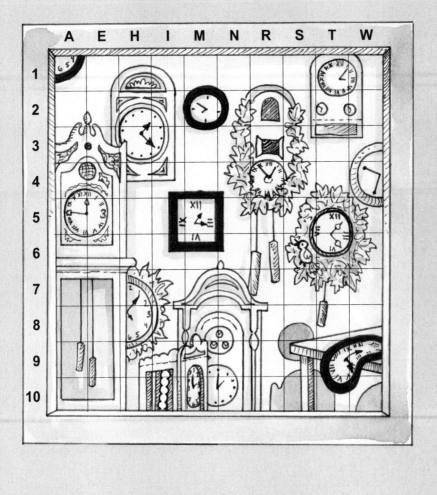

 $\overline{}$ $\overline{}$ $\overline{}$ $\overline{}$ $\overline{}$ $\overline{}$ $\overline{}$ $\overline{}$ $\overline{}$ $\overline{}$ $\overline{}$ $\overline{}$ $\overline{}$ $\overline{}$ $\overline{}$
 1 8 5   4 9 6 7 5 3   10 6   1 10 2 5

Big Mouth

Big Mouth can't keep a secret. Unfortunately, he also doesn't talk very clearly. He'll help you defeat the Shock, but only if you can figure out his crazy way of talking.

The strings of words below may look like nonsense, but actually each one is a clue to a common word. You'll have to say them out loud to make sense of them. For instance, say the words HATE TOUGH DIME HANDS FOUR HINTS TINTS, and you'll get "Eight of diamonds, for instance," a clue for the word CARD. It might help if you get somebody else to listen as you read each clue aloud.

Each pair of answers has exactly one letter in common. These four letters, in order, will give you the answer to this puzzle.

1.

SICKS TEAM INN HITS

EWE WRY TON DEB LAG BORED WIDTH HISS

2.

SILL FUR WHERE WIDTH ABLE AID

CULL LORE HUFF ATE HUM HAY TOE

3.

WAR TURF RUM THUS GUY

POSE DITCH SHAWN ANON FELL HOPE

4.

OUGHT TOME MOPE EEL

LIT HULL FEE MAIL

Captain Danger

Captain Danger likes putting people in danger, and he has to be stopped. Unfortunately, his hideout is this labyrinth pitted with traps. You'll need to summon up your courage to make it through.

Each numbered row has two clues. These answers will be written in order, one right after the other. There are also ten labyrinth clues. The answers to these clues will start in the upper left corner and follow the path until they emerge at the lower right corner. You'll have to figure out where each word starts and ends. When you're done, the circled letters, following along the labyrinth path, will spell out the answer to this puzzle.

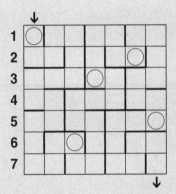

ROWS

1. Cook in the oven /
   Accomplished ("I ___ it!")
2. Basketball official, for short /
   Jump into the water headfirst
3. Soda flavor / Prolonged battle
4. Barbie's boyfriend / Large,
   round instrument you strike
   with a mallet
5. Flowery necklace you receive
   in Hawaii / Tiresome person
6. Separate into categories /
   Large body of water
7. Author Edgar Allan ___ / On
   its way, like mail

LABYRINTH

- Make unusable, like a toy
- Group of sheep
- Long, slippery kinds of fish
- Having the least money
- Game where you try to get
  five in a row
- Walk into the water
- What the ÷ symbol means
- "Home on the ___"
- Red flower
- Tidy

The Poet

Stealing isn't enough for the Poet—he then writes little rhyming riddles about the things he's taken. (He also steals a strange assortment of objects, as you'll soon see.) The Poet doesn't want to make things too easy for you, so he's deleted several words from each poem. These can all be seen in the box on the next page. Replace all the words, solve the riddles, and then take the letters from the white boxes to spell the solution to this puzzle.

1. Most people believe that I'm _____
   And on many a _____ I'm found.
   But here's an odd fact I will _____:
   _____ believe I am _____!

   ▢ __ __ __

2. Pull a _____ 'cross a string
   And I'm happy to ____.
   (A hint for this _____:
   I'm just like a _____.)

   __ __ ▢ __ __ __

3. Take one _____ of _____.
   And turn up the heat.
   Soon I'm _____ instead
   And _____ to eat.

   __ __ ▢ __ __

4. If the _____ is out,

   Just light up my _____.

   And before you can pout,

   it's _____ again _____!

   __ __ __ __ __ __ ▮

BOW

BOXERS

BREAD

BRIGHT

CRUNCHY

DELICIOUS

FIDDLE

FINGER

POWER

QUICK

RIDDLE

ROUND

SHARE

SING

SLICE

SQUARE

WICK

The Shock

It's time for the final showdown!

You now have five answers, one for each of the previous puzzles. First, write the answers in the spaces below so that each arrow points to an answer. Then write each letter into its corresponding numbered blank. When you're done, you'll spell out the secret trick to defeating the Shock!

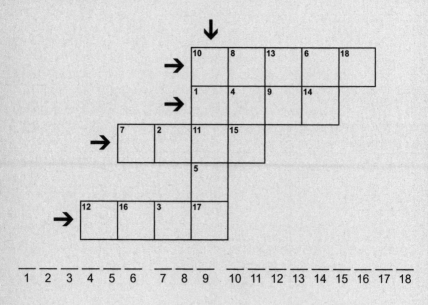

<u> </u> <u> </u> <u> </u> <u> </u> <u> </u> <u> </u>   <u> </u> <u> </u> <u> </u>   <u> </u> <u> </u> <u> </u> <u> </u> <u> </u> <u> </u> <u> </u> <u> </u> <u> </u>
1 2 3 4 5 6   7 8 9   10 11 12 13 14 15 16 17 18

ANSWERS

The Mad Zookeeper

CAMERA - RA + L = CAMEL

BADGE + R = BADGER

HOSE + R = HORSE

TIMER - M + G = TIGER

NAIL - A + O = LION

EASEL + W = WEASEL

FLOWER - ER = WOLF

DRIP - P + B = BIRD

STEAK - STE + Y = YAK

BONY → PONY

LIMB → LAMB

FIST → FISH

CREW → CROW

SEER → DEER

The answer to this puzzle is BITES.

Switcheroo

The letters spell out THE ANSWER IS TIME.

Big Mouth

SIXTY MINUTES = **H**OUR

YOU WRITE ON THE BLACKBOARD WITH THIS = **CH**ALK

SILVERWARE WITH A BLADE = KNIF**E**

COLOR OF A TOMATO = R**E**D

WATER FROM THE SKY = R**A**IN

POSTAGE ON AN ENVELOPE = ST**A**MP

AUTOMOBILE = CA**R**

LITTLE FEMALE = GI**R**L

The answer is HEAR.

Captain Danger

The answer is BRAVE.

The Poet

Most people believe that I'm round
And on many a finger I'm found.
But here's an odd fact I will share:
Boxers believe I am square!
R̲ING

Pull a bow 'cross a string
And I'm happy to sing.
(A hint for this riddle:
I'm just like a fiddle.)
VI̲OLIN

Take one slice of bread.
And turn up the heat.
Soon I'm crunchy instead
And delicious to eat.
TOA̲S̲T

If the power is out,
Just light up my wick.
And before you can pout,
it's bright again quick!
CANDL̲E̲

The answer is ROSE.

The Shock

The letters spell out REMOVE HIS BATTERIES.

ANSWERS

Page 3.

You can measure out 4 ounces of water in six moves:

1. Fill the 5-ounce beaker from the 8-ounce beaker.
2. Fill the 3-ounce beaker from the 5-ounce beaker. This will leave 2 ounces in the 5-ounce beaker.
3. Pour the 3-ounce beaker back into the 8-ounce beaker.
4. Pour the 2 ounces left in the 5-ounce beaker into the 3-ounce beaker.
5. Again fill the 5-ounce beaker from the 8-ounce beaker.
6. Fill the 3-ounce beaker from the 5-ounce beaker. Since there are 2 ounces already in the smallest beaker, you will need to add only 1 ounce to fill it, and this will leave you with 4 ounces in the 5-ounce beaker.

Page 8.

There are a number of possible answers, but here's one:

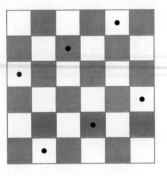

Pages 15–16.

1. Stack cats
2. Flee elf
3. Mirror rim
4. See referees
5. Nurses run
6. Bird rib
7. Panda had nap
8. Pupils slip up
9. Rise to vote, sir
10. Slap my gym pals

Page 19.

Scar / scarf

Slot / sloth

Crow / crown

Pear / pearl

Tub / tuba

Clam / clamp

Page 25.

Each number, when spelled out, has one more letter than the number before it. (ONE, FOUR, THREE, ELEVEN, and so on.) In each case, the first number with the correct number of letters is used. The next number in the series would be spelled with eleven letters; the first such number is TWENTY-THREE.

Pages 28–29.

MONSTER / MOBSTER
FIRE ANTS
NECTARINE / TOMATO / ONION
(FE)MALE
STENCH
CELLO
CHILLY / CHILI
TAP / PAT
NEW HAMPSHIRE

Page 35.

Page 52.

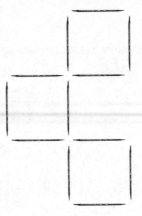

Page 54.

Page 75.

The three groups are as follows:

Titles where A is the only vowel: *All That Jazz, Avatar, Gattaca, Casablanca, Star Wars*

Titles that include a president's last name: *The Bridges of Madison County, Mr. Smith Goes to Washington, The Truman Show, Mildred Pierce, Arthur*

Titles with two words starting with the same letter: *Ella Enchanted, Mamma Mia!, Doctor Dolittle, Rob Roy, King Kong*

Page 94.

1 2 3 4 5 6 7 8 9 10   8 6 3 7 10 2 5 1 9 4

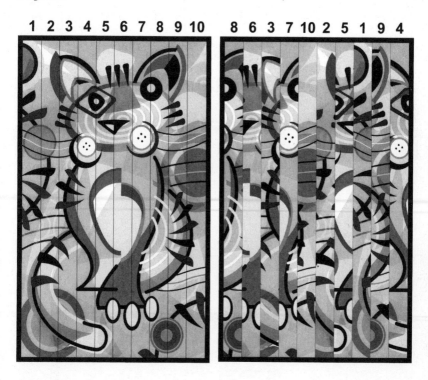

Page 101.

Page 107.

Orlando, Florida

Page 114.

1. Milk helps your bones grow, but I have to admit, so**da is yummier.**

2. Doris, Edwar**d, and Eli, on** their way to school, took a shortcut through the park.

3. After cleaning all the frying **pans, y**our next task will be to scrub the stove.

4. Snaps, zippers, laces, or Vel**cro? Cus**tom-made sneakers sure have a lot of options!

5. Once inside the cou**gar den, I a**wkwardly began taking pictures of the cubs.

Page 125.

Page 130.

DUMBER (add DRUM)
CAPTION (add PIANO)
GUNG-HO (add GONG)
GRANOLA (add ORGAN)
ORPHAN (add HARP)
JAWBONE (add BANJO)

RAVIOLI (add VIOLA)

BEAUTY (add TUBA)

Pages 142–143.

MENTION and MONTANA

AVERAGE and VIRGO

PIANISSIMO and OPEN SESAME

AFTER and FUTURE

EAGLE and GOALIE

OREGON and REIGN

TALENT and ATLANTA

INTERN and NEUTRON

LOBSTER and ALABASTER

AISLE and USUAL

OCARINA and ACORN

PRINCESS and HEADGEAR are left over.

Page 222.